Front cover illustration by Jim Agpalza

Edited by Matthew A. Clarke

SHITHOLE USA

Mark Zirbel

Planet Bizarro Press

GREETINGS FROM FLORIDA ...

OCTOBER 5TH, 2:42 PM – An emergency meeting of SOIL, the Syndicate of Intelligence Liaisons, is called to order. All of the usual suspects are in attendance, including current and former CIA spooks, a pair of well-dressed Panamanian hitmen, sentient slabs of Russian beef hanging from meat hooks, a Chinese supercomputer, Count Dracula, and the cybercryo head of Dick Cheney. Due to a scheduling mishap, they're crammed around a U-shaped conference table at the airport Ramada in Boise. A cute little polio-stricken boy hobbles to the front of the room; propped up with leg braces and crutches, he sings "God Bless America." After a polite round of applause, it's time to get down to the business at hand: an update on the Advanced Neurosyphilis Infection Syndrome (ANSIS) crisis in Florida. They start by going around the table for quick-fire updates from SOIL's subject matter experts. Doctor Harry Dickinsider, the porn star turned world-renowned microbiologist, kicks things off.

(Fun Fact: Several members of SOIL have made the mistake of checking out the doctor's old movies, and they now find it impossible to listen to him speak without thinking about his massive, throbbing, cum-spurting cock.)

"My team has been working around the clock," Dickinsider says, "and we now have conclusive data to support our initial suspicions about ANSIS. It's an advanced and mutated form of syphilis resistant to any known treatments. It's sexually transmitted like its progenitor. Those infected exhibit symptoms associated with the final stage of syphilis. This occurs within days rather than years or decades, as would normally be the case. The most noticeable symptom is the eruption of tumor-like balls of inflammation, known as gummas, all over the body. ANSIS also infects the central nervous system, resulting in confusion, aggression, and extreme hypersexuality. That's why the disease is continuing to spread so quickly throughout Florida. Everyone is, well, fucking each other's brains out, basically."

There's a murmur of chuckles in the room.

Brigadier General Regis Marcel pounds his fist on the table. "You think this is funny? It's no joke to my men on the front line!"

"Is the Florida border still secured, General?" one of the Panamanians asks.

"We've increased our border presence to more than three hundred thousand troops, representing over half of the active U.S. Army. To put it bluntly, nobody is getting out of that godforsaken state. ANSIS is contained."

"Umm, General?" the Panamanian says. "Do you mind if I ask? Your teeth ...?"

The General's upper and lower incisors are triangle-shaped and pointed, like the teeth of a piranha.

"I filed them down. If one of those sex-crazed mutants tries to feed me some salami, they'll be in for a surprise!"

"I thought you said the border is secure."

"It is! For now. But if those bastards ever have the presence of mind to attack our troops *en masse,* we'll be in trouble. We need to be prepared for the worst. Check this out ..."

The General stands up, unfastens his belt, and drops his brown dress slacks to the floor. He's wearing an odd-looking pair of underwear, kind of like a leather jock strap, but with a little cage attached that's holding his penis in place.

"This is a chastity belt for men. I got it in a queer shop in L.A. There's a dick cage in front and a butt plug in the back. Between this and my sharpened teeth, *my* entry points are secure."

More chuckles.

"Stop laughing!"

"All right, you imbeciles. Enough of this horseshit." Despite being confined to a wheelchair, Beauford Tinker commands the attention of everyone in the room. Years ago, he led a First Response Assault Team in the Army. Tinker and his FRAT boys used to give America's crybaby protestors something *serious* to cry about! Since becoming a paraplegic, he's headed up one of the world's most feared private intelligence outfits. "Let's talk about the World Village. That's why we're all here today, isn't it?"

(Fun Fact: With an area of nearly three thousand square miles, the World Village is the largest retirement community in the U.S. The thirty-foot-high concrete wall surrounding the property stretches across central Florida's Sumter, Lake, and Orange Counties.)

"There haven't been any breaches in the wall," Tinker continues, "so the residents of the World Village are going on with their lives like ANSIS doesn't exist. Pretty goddamned convenient that Peora finished building his wall right before the outbreak started, wouldn't you say?"

"Are you suggesting that the president of World Village Incorporated is somehow responsible for the ANSIS epidemic?" Dickinsider asks.

"I don't know what I'm suggesting because I don't have enough intel. With the resources at my disposal, I could find out what you ate for breakfast on the day you lost your virginity, Dickinsider. And yet I can't get one goddamned piece of info about Alfred Peora. Nothing! I don't know if he's your basic business tycoon, a politico, or some Charles Manson type. I'm starting to wonder if he's nothing but a cyberghost."

"We need someone on the inside," the General says.

"Thanks, General Obvious. I've put together a plan to do just that. We have to move fast on this, especially in light of yesterday's hocus pocus. I'll discuss that incident in a minute, but needless to say, it's imperative to know if Peora was involved. Somebody dim the overheads."

The room goes dark, and the multimedia screen at the front of the room lights up. The title slide of the presentation reads:

OPERATION CHOCOLATE STARFISH

TOP SECRET/CONFIDENTIAL

FOR SOIL EYES ONLY

IF YOU VIEW THIS PRESENTATION AND ARE NOT A MEMBER OF SOIL, YOU ARE HEREBY INSTRUCTED TO KILL YOURSELF IMMEDIATELY

FAILURE TO COMPLY WILL RESULT IN A CONSIDERABLY MORE BRUTAL DEATH AT THE HANDS OF SOIL OPERATIVES

"Did the cripple leave the room?" Tinker asks. "Yeah? Good. It would be a shame to have to put the little guy down. He's got the voice of an angel.

"Okay, ladies. Everybody shut your cornholes and pay attention.

"Next slide ..."

PART I: CONFLUENCE

TekCircle's career development framework is built upon the Lioli Principle, named after our CEO, Hugh Lioli. Lioli firmly believes that if you don't love your job, something is wrong—and that "something" is probably you. Perhaps you're not fully committed to learning, growing, and excelling on a daily basis. At TekCircle, we won't let you let yourself down. The first three years of your employment will be spent at one of our workcamps, where you'll be immersed in our exciting and fast-paced corporate culture. You'll live and breathe our commitment to excellence, 24x7. After three years, you're welcome to move off-site, but why would you want to? At TekCircle, you're already home.

-- From the Careers page of TekCircle's website

CHAPTER 1

My day begins like any other at workcamp, with an auditory hallucination. A sharp, horrible clanging rattles me awake, like a wind-up metal woodpecker has been set loose inside my skull. I hit my mental snooze button. It's a reflexive move, my brain's way of putting off the waking hell that awaits me. The noise that was never there stops.

"Gimme ten minutes," I mumble.

Come on, Ryan. Ten more minutes of sleep aren't going to make a difference.

The little voice in my head is always so sensible.

If you go back to sleep, you'll feel even more tired when you get up.

It's a woman's voice—soothing, reassuring.

You know what's going to happen. Hit snooze once, and you'll end up hitting it five more times.

She's right.

You can't afford to be late for work again.

She has my back.

So how about you hop out of bed and start your day the TekCircle way!

Aw, fuck.

When I'm half asleep, it's easy to get swept along with her. But she usually trips herself up with some company BS. And then I remember what's really in my head.

A corporate parasite.

TEKCIRCLE EMPLOYEES FEELING 'CHIPPER' ABOUT MANDATORY RFID IMPLANTS

That was the headline of the company-issued press release. It got heavy coverage, with lots of feel-good quotes from the top brass.

Barbara Blade, Director of HR: "The procedure takes only seconds, with a microchip safely and easily imbedded just beneath the skin of an employee's forehead."

That part was true. The instrument they used looked like a bolt gun for stunning cattle. Muzzle to the head, pull the trigger. Wham, bam, done. Next!

Jeff Lord, Chief Operating Officer: "On-premises chip scanners will enable TekCircle employees to open doors, log into their computers, and more, without ever having to carry a badge or memorize a passcode. It's all about creating a faster and easier work experience for our employees."

Yeah, it's great. I can buy a bag of corn nuts in the company cafeteria without taking out my wallet.

(On a side note: TekCircle's microchips acted as the delivery device for some sort of nanotech organism, a tiny critter that's burrowed its way deep into the cerebrum of each and every employee.)

PROJECT HIVEMIND HAS TEKCIRCLE EMPLOYEES 'BUZZING' WITH EXCITEMENT

Another press release, more warm-and-fuzzy quotes.

Andrew Powers, Vice Chairman and President: "We're excited to announce a bold new way to combine TekCircle's people power and computing power, harnessing the full potential of our collective intelligence."

Lester Steel, Chief Technology Officer: "We drew our inspiration from honeybees—colony workers serving their queen in a system of perfect unity. Using state-of-the-art cyber insectoids, we're bringing that same type of swarm sensibility to TekCircle."

With Project Hivemind, you're never alone, not even with your thoughts. Your little PAL (Parietal Autonomous Link) is always with you. It can wake you up at the exact crack of dawn with an imaginary alarm clock in your head. Or give you motivational pep talks throughout the day.

What do you say, Ryan? Should we start our day the TekCircle way?

Sure, why not? Let's get this shitshow going.

"Cancel snooze."

I throw my thin, scratchy blanket aside and swing my legs out of bed. My feet hit the carpet with a wet squish, and a sharp tang fills my nostrils.

The area around my cot is soaked in urine.

This has to be the handiwork of Christina Draco, TekCircle's Director of Strategic Account Development. Why do so many people in the corporate world feel the need to mark their territory? Christina has made it clear that she wants to bring my training team under her sales umbrella. There was a time when I would've fought the move, but I don't care anymore. I'm not in the mood for a pissing match.

My cube-mate, Keerin, is already out of bed and sitting at his desk, drinking a cup of coffee, looking all knobby-kneed in his underwear. He's straight out of high school, but with his lanky frame, buzzcut, and company-issued Birth Control Glasses, he could pass for thirteen. TekCircle keeps hiring them younger and younger—it makes me feel like a senior citizen at forty-three. So long as the kid doesn't make it worse by calling me—

"Good morning, sir."

Aw, fuck.

"Ryan," I say, correcting him for the ten-thousandth time. I point to the pee-stained carpet. "Guess the Dragon Lady paid me a visit last night, huh? Must've snuck over from the Women's Wing."

"Yeah, and that's not all. Frankie and his crew did a number on you, too."

"What do you mean?"

"Your face."

I open my battered foot locker and grab a hand mirror. A graffiti-covered Satan stares back at me. "What the ...!"

A devil's mustache and beard have been drawn on me with a thick, black marker. The word PENIS is scrawled across my forehead. My left cheek says I'M A FAG. On my right cheek, a cartoon dick is ejaculating cum circles at my mouth.

Frankie Strong and his gang of corporate bullies have struck again.

"Are you fucking kidding me? I've got an integration meeting with Cybersquare today."

"I'm sure that's why they did it," Keerin says. He opens his desk drawer and takes out a bottle of rubbing alcohol. "Here, help yourself. It's left over from when they nailed me last month. Right before my big presentation at the QBR."

I look at the instructions on the label. "This'll take care of it?"

"It helps. But it'll be a couple of days before the ink fades completely."

"Great. Just great."

"Sorry. Oh, hey—here's something to cheer you up. Or give you a chuckle, at least." Keerin pulls up a news story on his computer. "Check this out."

I get up and read the headline over his shoulder:

FLORIDA ZOMBIE ATTACKS BORDER GUARD WHILE SODOMIZING ARMADILLIO

Keerin bursts out laughing. "Can you believe that?"

What I really find hard to believe is that some news outlets are calling the infected "zombies." They're acting like ANSIS is a big joke! Just because the military has the disease contained within Florida, the rest of us can sit back and have a good laugh? What's wrong with people?

"I don't think those Florida Zombie stories are very funny," I say.

Keerin shoots me a wary look. "You're not one of those Zels, are you?"

A Zel is a Zombie Lover (Zel, as in ZL). A snowflake who has sympathy for the infected. Someone who thinks the Army should airlift supplies into Florida while we search for a cure for ANSIS, instead of letting the state fuck itself to death.

I sigh. "No, I'm not one of *those.* It's just ... My mom is down there, and I'm kind of worried about her."

"She's in *Florida?*"

"In the World Village. She flew down yesterday to visit a friend."

"Oh ... *OH!* She should be fine then. Those zombies aren't getting in *there!*"

"I know. But I don't like her travelling alone. She said she would check in with me last night, and I didn't hear from her."

"She's probably too busy ... you know. Getting laid."

"Whoa ... Fuck, man!"

Keerin starts laughing again. "I'm only kidding. There *are* a lot of swingers in the World Village, though. All kinds of orgies and wife swapping and stuff. Tons of STDs, too. I've even heard that ANSIS might have started there."

"That's bullshit."

"No, seriously. They're saying a resident had this pet chimp, and he'd doll it up with a wig and makeup, and his war buddies would come over and do the spunky monkey. Three bucks apiece. And then pretty soon their dicks started falling off, and—"

"None of that stuff's true, Keerin! Jesus."

"Are you sure you're not a Zel? You're awfully sensitive."

"I'm concerned about my mom. I don't need to hear a bunch of World Village horror stories."

"Sorry."

"If she doesn't call by noon ..."

"She'll call, she'll call. Don't worry about it. You better go clean yourself up, sir."

I put on my robe and flip-flops and head to the bathroom. The aisle of cubicles is long—assclowns to the left of me, brown-nosers to the right. Most of my co-workers are already up and at 'em, ready for another day of sales and subterfuge. Capitalist drones in black latex bodysuits. It started as a joke. We're Sales & Marketing—S&M—we should all wear bondage outfits. Hahaha. Not known for their sense of humor, executive management loved the idea. And not only for Sales & Marketing. For the whole company.

TEKCIRCLE EMPLOYEES 'SUBMIT' TO ENTHUSIASM OVER NEW COMPANY UNIFORMS

Yes, another goddamned press release.

Stephanie Worth, Chief Financial Officer: "Simply put, latex feels sensational. It's sleek and sexy and has our employees brimming with confidence. Imagine having a staff that's 40-50% more self-assured than the competition. That's going to have a positive impact on our bottom line."

Rich Moore, Chief Investment Officer: "Our employees are our fuck-toy slaves, so why not dress them that way?"

The company caught some heat for that last quote, but it blew over in less than a week.

Oh, and the head of PR was fired.

When I enter the bathroom, someone grunts in the third stall like they're giving birth. I wish I knew who's in there. If it's one of Frankie's crew, it would be best to come back later. As bad as the bullying gets in the office, it's even worse in the john. It's like a cross between *Riot in Cell Block 11* and *Lord of the Flies* in here. Is it something about the ripe stink of shit that does it? Does it unleash a primal rage? Whatever the case, I decide to roll the dice and tend to my face.

No sooner do I step in front of the sink and mirror than the stall door opens behind me. It's not a member of Frankie's crew. No, just my luck, it's FUCKING FRANKIE HIMSELF. He gives me a chip-toothed grin as he exits the stall without flushing. This kid *never* flushes. His turds are someone else's problem.

"Well, if it isn't Cryin' Ryan," Frankie says. "Nice makeup."

He's looking for a fight that he knows I won't give him. He and his crew are tripwire bombs ready to explode, packed with teenage muscle and bad intent. Best I can do is say, "Leave me alone."

Frankie moves up to the sink next to mine. "Or, *what?* Are you gonna go crying to HR again?"

No, I learned my lesson after the RhomBiz merger closed last year. Frankie's crew was celebrating in the War Room. Champagne, whores. There was *no way* those girls were eighteen. I just thought someone should know. Turns out they were company girls—adopted by TekCircle, raised on hardcore porn. The report I filed using the company's anonymous whistleblower website was traced back to my computer. I got a ton of static from management and the nickname Cryin' Ryan. Since then,

I've learned to keep my mouth shut and do my job, no matter what I see or hear. The bullying hasn't stopped, though.

"Hey, are you a Homo sapien?" Frankie asks.

I ignore him.

Frankie takes a step closer to me. His shiny latex uniform stinks of silicone spray and B.O. "Fucking. Answer. Me."

"Fine. Yes."

"Yes, *what?*"

"Yes, I'm a Homo—"

"I knew it!" Frankie shouts, cutting me off. "I knew you were a homo. You even admitted it. Ha! Wait till I tell the guys."

Whoa ... freeze frame! This dingus is in the PERFECT spot to nail him with a knee stomp.

Come again? My PAL is back, but what the hell is she talking about?

"I swear, Cryin' Ryan, you're the biggest faggot loser in this whole company!"

I could talk you through it, but it'd be a lot easier if you gave me control.

Umm ...

"How did you get to be such a loser? C'mon, Cryin' Ryan. I really want to know."

I'm gonna grab the wheel, okay?

I ... guess ...?

Perfect.

{TAKEOVER SEQUENCE:\ -> tempIndex,,,:/gateway/ body.mind; >>>_run_}

Okay, here we go. The move is like kicking a soccer ball, except you're aiming for your opponent's kneecap. Whamo-blamo! Franke's left leg buckles on contact, and he crashes face-first to the floor. Look at him there—lying on his belly, groaning in his bodysuit. Kinda reminds me of a sea lion. *Arf-arf-arf!* Too funny! ANY-hoo ... I reach down and grab a handful of his hair.

Jeez, it's like a Brillo pad! I've heard you shouldn't use a Brillo pad to clean your toilet bowl. They say it's too abrasive.

Let's find out if that's true.

I drag Frankie back into the stall and shove his face into the mess he left behind. When I let him up, wet toilet paper clings to his face. Oh my god, he looks like a mummy. A dookie mummy! He gasps for air and sucks a brown streak right into his mouth. Gross! He coughs and gags and I shove his head back into the water—all the way down—right into the mush at the bottom. When I let him up this time, it looks like he's taken a cow pie to the face. There's crap in his eyes, up his nose, and all around his mouth. *Ugh*—he reeks! I lift him to his feet and toss him the fuck away from me, which makes him stumble backwards and clonk his head on the floor. I feel like I should stand over him and give a speech about how a bully never wins in the end, blah-blah-blah. But he wouldn't even hear me. He's too busy puking and blowing shit rockets out of his nose! Doesn't matter—a wounded animal knows when it's beat. Frankie and his crew are done.

{TAKEOVER SEQUENCE:\ -> abort.command = </pri-ority1>; // >>>_shutdown_}

Back over to you, Ryan. Thanks!

What ... happened? I feel like I've woken up from a dream. No, that's not right. It's more like I was watching television. A first-person POV TV show starring ... me. But with my PAL playing the lead role. Except it wasn't really my PAL. I mean, since when does my PAL use words like *dingus?* Her voice was the same, but her personality was different. Is my PAL schizophrenic? Am *I?* I'd like to pretend that the whole thing never happened, but that's hard to do with Frankie curled into a fetal position on the floor, crying with shit smeared all over his face. I really fucked him up.

Jesus ... What's happening to me?

CHAPTER 2

Hank Shatley settles back in his recliner and takes a sip of whiskey, letting it engulf his tongue for a moment before swallowing the burn.

"Craft bourbon?" he grumbles. "More like crap bourbon."

Hank recalls a quote from Raymond Chandler: "There is no bad whiskey. There are only some whiskeys that aren't as good as others." Easy for him to say. Back in RC's day, there wasn't a boutique distillery in every city, run by hipster giraffes with their tattooed spots and neck-stretching rings. The whiskey Hank is drinking was a retirement gift from the boys at the station. It came in a fancy little bottle and cost a hundred bucks. He takes another sip.

"Christ. Like turpentine with cinnamon."

The batch was probably rapid-aged by an MIT chemist. It amazes Hank that so many people fail to understand such a simple truth: Some things take time.

Time. Hank has plenty of it now, retired at fifty-five. With his trim physique and spiky brown hair, he could pass for forty-five. But he just couldn't deal with the job anymore—and all the shit that went along with it. There was the endless political BS, the winks and secret handshakes, constantly being prodded to attend those power breakfasts with the Chief.

Gotta play ball if you wanna make lieutenant, Hank.

Cram it.

And then there was the actual shit. The hot sloppies. About thirty percent of stiffs crap themselves. That might sound like a low percentage, but it's plenty high for a homicide dick with a thing about poo. Every time Hank arrived at a crime scene, his number-one priority was to sniff for number two. If he caught a whiff of it, he made sure he stayed as far away from the corpse as possible. It's not like he needed to get down and dirty with it; that's what the forensics guys were there for. But his mind would start racing, and he'd imagine a scenario where he'd get some of the brown stuff on him. Maybe Jensen from the crime lab unit would toss a poopy rubber glove at him for a laugh. Just the thought of it made Hank feel like a rabid jackrabbit was trying to kick its way out of his chest. The panic attacks got bad enough that he decided to give the department therapist a whirl. The shrink said that Hank had fecal contamination OCD—in layman's terms, an unnatural fear of coming in contact with excrement. He recommended a treatment regimen in which Hank would expose himself to more and more poo each day until he was desensitized to it. Hank recommended that the shrink go fuck himself.

Hank isn't sure what's next for him. He doesn't plan to sit on his duff forever. But for now, he's content to enjoy some downtime in his den. It's his favorite room in the house, filled with sports memorabilia, crime-flick movie posters, and vintage bar games. Most importantly, it's his designated safe zone. This means that no one else is allowed in the den—ever! Hank won't go inside, either, until he's completed his compulsory ritual:

STEP 1: Hank strips and tosses all his clothes down the laundry chute in the hallway.

STEP 2: Hank showers in the hall bathroom. He washes his butt last to avoid contaminating the rest of his body.

STEP 3: After drying himself with a clean towel, Hank dresses in fresh clothes from the linen closet (he uses it as a clothes closet, so he doesn't have to walk to the bedroom and risk contamination).

STEP 4: Hank can go into the den and enjoy himself, knowing that both he and the room are doody-free.

With whiskey warming his belly, Hank figures that a nap is inevitable. He reclines his chair all the way back and closes his eyes. A moment later, his home intercom system is chiming. It's the middle of the afternoon, so it has to be a solicitor or someone Hank doesn't want to talk to (which includes just about everyone). A voice comes through: "Shitley! Open the goddamned door! I know you're in there!"

Shitley?

Nobody's called him that since—

Hank springs from his chair and races out of the den, down the hall, to the front door. He opens the door to reveal a man in a wheelchair, dressed in a suit and tie. He looks so different—bald, heavy, jowly—but it has to be him.

"Sarge?"

"Do you see three stripes on my sleeve?" the man asks. "Well? Do you?"

"No ..."

"Then what are you calling me *Sarge* for? Don't be an imbecile."

Hank can't believe he's being derided like a grunt. If anyone else talked to him like this, they'd be flat on their back, seeing stars. But Hank wouldn't be here if it wasn't for this ornery SOB. The guy saved his life back when Hank was a FRAT boy in the Army.

"So ...? Are you gonna invite me in?"

Hank hesitates, his eyes darting to the wheels on his former sergeant's chair.

"What's the problem? I didn't come from the goddamned dog park!"

Hank feels his face flush with embarrassment. "No, of course not. Come on in, Sar— Err, I mean ... What do I call you now? Beauford?"

"Call me that, and it'll be the last fucking word you utter. I guess Sarge will do, since you seem to have your precious heart set on it."

"How long's it been?"

"Thirty years, Shitley. Thirty years since I saw you. Thirty years in this cripple-mobile."

Hank feels lower than dirt. He struggles for something to say. The best he can manage is ridiculously inadequate: "I'm sorry, Sarge."

"No apologies! I told you that back then, and the same's true now. There's blame all around. I knew you had poop issues, and what did I do? I sent you into a riot zone full of shit slingers. Not my smartest command decision."

All these years later, Hank can still feel the splash of the water balloon on his face. Except it wasn't filled with water. Hank's unit was facing off against the Brown Underground, a group of radical performance artists and self-proclaimed turd terrorists. Fight shit with shit. That was their motto. They were famous for hurling sewage-filled balloons at their enemies, including CEOs, politicians, cops, and FRAT boys. Hank had never tasted poop before, obviously, but he knew that's what it was, that horrible sludge in his mouth. He expected to puke but froze instead. Combat paralysis. Caca paralysis. He couldn't get himself to move, not even when the rioter who threw the balloon pulled a gun. Hank would be dead if Sarge hadn't leaped in front of him.

"I suspect things worked out for the best. For both of us," Sarge says.

Hank is stunned by this comment. "What do you mean?"

"If it wasn't for my disability, I would've ended up being a lifer in the Army. Never would've started my own company, which I love. And you never seemed very happy in the FRAT. Were you?"

"No."

"How come?"

"I don't know. Busting people's heads for protesting? It wasn't really my thing."

"Huh! I *loved* that part of the job! Oh, well ... The point is that you became one hell of a detective. I've followed your career. Medals and commendations from here to Timbuktu."

"Yeah, well ..."

"This is a nice place you have," Sarge says, changing the subject. Using a joystick device on his wheelchair, he cruises down the hall and stops in front of the den. "What's this? A game room? Ooh—foosball!" He heads on in.

Hank wants to shout—*NOOOOOOOOOOOO!!!*—but he stifles himself and follows Sarge into his one and only contamination-free room.

"Sweet setup," Sarge says as he fiddles with the foosball handles, spinning the red men around.

"Something I can do for you?" Hank does his best to sound casual, but his inner OCD voice is firing off a barrage of questions: *Did you take a shit today, Sarge? Did you wash your hands? Did you use hot and soapy water? For how long?*

Sarge wheels himself to the pool table and runs his fingers over the felt. "Here's the skinny, Shitley. I own a private intelligence firm. We're investigating reports of a paranormal occurrence in the World Village. It happened last week, during a big outdoor concert."

Hank is trying hard to keep it together. "Yeah? Who was playing?"

"Chocolate Starfish," Sarge says, taking a pool cue from the rack. "They're a Limp Bizkit cover band."

"Right." *(Gonna have to wipe everything down.)*

Sarge replaces the cue and checks out another one. "Halfway through the band's second encore—I think it was 'Nookie'—a huge glowing orb appeared in front of the stage."

"Uh-huh." *(Do I have enough disinfectant?)*

"People thought it was part of the show, some kind of laser effect. But when the fireball disappeared, a young woman was standing in its place. Eighteen to twenty-three years old. Purple mohawk. Naked as a jaybird and covered in tattoos. She was disoriented, talking nonsense. Something about needing to wake up. Gotta wake up! Gotta wake up! That's what she kept shouting. The police showed up and hauled her away."

Hank holds his breath as Sarge heads over to his Neon City pinball machine. It's his all-time favorite.

No ... c'mon ... please ...

Sarge pulls the lever and slaps the flipper buttons a few times.

"CHRIST! DO YOU HAVE TO TOUCH FUCKING EVERYTHING?"

Sarge looks bewildered by Hank's outburst—and then it hits him. "My god. Shitley! You *still* have poop issues? I was only kidding with my dog park remark. I figured you got help decades ago. You said you would."

"I didn't, okay? But I'm fine."

"*Fine?* Look at you. You're a walking sweat rag! It's time to deal with this. My assignment will be perfect for you."

"Huh? What assignment?"

"I need an inside man. ANSIS has turned the World Village into a country onto itself, and nobody knows who's running the show. On paper it's Alfred Peora, the president of World

Village Incorporated. But his identity is a fabricated dead end. The guy's a total mystery. The conjuring act at the concert has the intelligence community worried he's fooling around with corporate chaos magic."

Hank hates all that corpo alakazam. These Ivy League assholes can't stretch their profit margins enough with dirty tricks and backroom deals? They need to resort to sorcery? Still, it's none of his business. "I care because ...?"

"I don't have any field agents who are fifty-five-plus. You're the right age. You've got the right skill set. And, quite frankly, you owe me one." Sarge pats his dead legs.

"You said no apologies!"

"I don't want an apology. I want you to take this assignment."

"What was that about it being perfect for me?"

"It's the goddamndest thing. People in the World Village have gone coo-coo for poo-poo. They're making pottery with it in their art classes. Getting massaged with it at the spa. Eating a schmear of it with onions on a slice of rye."

That last one pushes Hank over the edge. His throat burns as he retches his bourbon, sending a hot gush splashing to the floor. Hands on his knees, Hank tries to pull himself together. "How the hell's that perfect?"

"You'll be forced to face your fear—and safely. There won't be anyone shooting at you this time."

"No way. I can't."

"Man up, Shitley. You've spent your life trying to outrun a landslide. A landslide of butt mud! No more running. Let me show you something."

Sarge unbuttons the bottom of his shirt and lifts it. There's a pouch of some sort resting against his hip. Hank's first thought is that it's a hot water bottle.

"This is my shit sack," Sarge says, unzipping his pants so he can get at the colostomy bag.

Now that Hank has a better look at it, he can see the slop inside. Just a thin layer of plastic between him and the bad brown *thang*. He can feel his heart rate revving up.

Sarge pulls the bag off his body, exposing a small, bright-red protuberance on his abdomen. "Meet Stevie. Stevie the Stoma."

The opening in the tip of the stoma moves like a tiny mouth and says, "Nice ta meetcha!" It's the voice of a child, a 1930s ragamuffin.

Hank's revulsion gives way to confusion. "It ... talks?"

"It was an expensive procedure," Sarge says. "But Uncle Sam was footing the bill, so I figured what the hell."

The stoma pipes in: "Yeah! What the H-E double toothpicks!"

"Thirty years ago, I didn't think I could handle having to clean Stevie every day. But look at us now."

"We's the most bestest pals," Stevie says. "Maybe you and me could be pals too, Mr. Hank. I ain't such a bad egg. And the Sarge needs ya big-time. Whadaya say? Can'tcha help us out?"

"Well, look. I don't—"

"Pweeez?"

Dammit. This kind of stuff always gets to Hank. Poor wretches like Oliver Twist and Tiny Tim. That *"God bless us, every one"* line makes him cry every time. Stevie reminds him of the tikes in those children's hospital commercials. *("Won't you make a dream come true for a little knucklehead like me?")* Hanks wants to give and give generously to Stevie. He wants to give till it hurts. He wants to give *right now!* Maybe it's easier for Hank to feel sympathy for a nub of conscious tissue than to face what he did to Sarge. The man has been bound to a wheelchair for half his life, denied so much, even the basic dignity of normal bowel movements. Dealing with some blue-hairs with a poop fetish is nothing compared to that. Like Sarge said, it's time to man up. "Okay, okay. Christ. I'll do it."

Stevie is jubilant. "Yaaaaaaaaaay!"

"You're a good man, Shitley. We need to get you in shape, though. Can't have you flipping out down there. Time for some exposure therapy." Sarge runs his fingers across the colostomy bag, applying pressure like a tube of toothpaste, squeezing out a foul-smelling brown glob onto the freshly shampooed carpet.

Hank stares in horror, mouth agape. It feels like his brain is burning. Charred bubbles spread across his field of vision. He struggles to say something through tingling nausea.

Sarge points at the sullied floor. "Clean that up, Shitley. Chop-chop!"

CHAPTER 3

Nobody in the conference room says a word about the vulgar graffiti on my face.

Representatives from both Cybersquare and TekCircle are in attendance, so it's a mix of business suits and fetish gear in the seating gallery. I can't believe that none of my TekCircle colleagues laugh or point when I go up to the podium. As I begin my presentation, people seem more attentive than usual. For the first time in a long time, not a single spitball is shot at me, and when I turn around to write on the whiteboard, the room doesn't break out in farting noises.

The end of my training update is met with a round of applause, which has never happened before. I even get a few handshakes, back slaps, and nice-jobs. What's the deal? I'm guessing that word of my run-in with Frankie has gotten around the office. Do my colleagues hate the kid as much as I do? Everyone files out immediately, so I don't have a chance to ask questions.

I walk over to the conference room's giant windows and take in the 150th-floor view of downtown Chicago: a panorama of skyscrapers strung together with suicide nets. On the street below, a hundred or so members of SHART (Satan-Haters

Against RFID Technology) are at it again. I can't see what their signs say from up here, but I'm sure it's the typical stuff.

ARMAGEDDON = BIG PROFITS

THE END IS NEAR! TEKCIRCLE IS THE PUPPETTER!

CORPORATE DEVILS BURN IN HELL

These loonies have been protesting here every day, wearing poop emoji masks and carrying assault weapons, ever since TekCircle announced its employee microchipping program. They're convinced that the End of Days is at hand and that TekCircle is responsible for it because of some passage in the Bible. Something about all men receiving a mark on their foreheads, and nobody will be able to buy or sell without that mark. It's from the Book of Revelation, I think. Considering it was written almost two thousand years ago, there *are* some eerie parallels with the idea of human microchipping. But come on ... The chip in my forehead is the mark of Satan? That's ridiculous! There *is* something weird going on with it, though. Well, maybe the chip itself is fine. The PAL that it launched into my brain, that's another story. I wish I could ask Keerin if his PAL has ever acted up like this. But employees aren't supposed to discuss their PALs with each other. Everything we need to know about our PALs was covered in a set of corporate FAQs. Using my PAL's recall function, I can pull them up in my head anytime I want.

{ARCHIVE:\ -> KnowledgeTransferId = <parietal_autonomous_link_-_frequently_asked_questions>; >>>_run_}

Q. I started hearing a voice inside my head. Am I going crazy?

A. No, that's your PAL talking to you.

Q. What's a PAL?

A. PAL stands for Parietal Autonomous Link. It's a cybernetic system that resides in the Parietal Lobe of your brain.

Q. How did it get there?

A. As you know, all TekCircle employees are required to have an RFID chip embedded in their forehead. That chip, in addition to simplifying your life in innumerable ways, also served as the staging area for your PAL. With the announcement of Project Hivemind, all PALs were activated and deployed company-wide.

Q. What's Project Hivemind?

A. For the complete details, turn your thoughts to the press release:

{ARCHIVE:\ -> KnowledgeTransferId = <project_hivemind_has_tekcircle_employees_'buzzing'_with_excitement>; >>>_run_}

The simple answer is that Project Hivemind is a strategy for connecting TekCircle with its employees—to get us all following the same playbook—using highly advanced cyborg insects.

Q. I have a bug in my brain?

A. So to speak. Your PAL is a special type of robotic bug known as a nanite. It's an innovative form of micro artificial intelligence.

Q. Micro? How small is it?

A. Think about it this way: Your RFID chip is about the size of a grain of rice. By comparison, your PAL isn't even visible to the human eye. You'd need a very powerful microscope to see it. However, that tiny PAL of yours can make a huge difference in your career!

Q. How can my PAL help me?

A. Your PAL is a mentor who's there to guide you to success at TekCircle. Throughout the day, your PAL will offer you tips on how to work smarter and more productively.

Q. Are all PALs the same?

A. Not at all! Your PAL will tap into your inner self and present itself to you in a way that's best suited to your personality.

It could be an authoritative man, a soft-spoken woman, or a million other possibilities, each one as unique and special as you. Whatever form your PAL takes, be sure to take advantage of the tremendous learning opportunities. Your PAL is always looking out for your best interests.

Q. Are there any risks associated with my PAL?

A. Nothing is more important than the health and wellbeing of our employees. You can rest assured that your PAL is completely safe. In fact, following the advice of your PAL makes you ten times more likely to be promoted, so the only danger is to our executives. Before long, you might be taking one of their jobs!

What a crock of... Eh, I better not go there. Thanks to my PAL, there's no such thing as a private thought anymore. The FAQs skipped right over *that* point, that a PAL is like having corporate spyware in your head, sending constant transmissions of your brain's data to HQ. But that's what's so weird about what happened to me this morning. *TekCircle knows.* They know that my PAL's personality changed. They know she took control of me. They know she made me beat the crap out of Frankie. And they're fine with it. That rules out a defect in the system. If they thought there was something wrong with my PAL, I'd be in the Employee OR having brain surgery right now. TekCircle must be planning to demote Frankie or maybe even fire him. The question is, why was I chosen to take him down a notch? Was I a random lackey? Or, after all these years, has management identified me as a high-potential employee?

My phone hums from the top of the podium where I left it (no pockets in this stupid gimp suit). I walk to the podium, and when I pick up my phone, it displays an unknown 352 (Florida) number. Mom?

I swipe the Answer icon: "Hello?"

"Ryan?"

"Mom! Is everything okay?"

"Of course, dear. Why wouldn't it be?"

"You never called me last night. And why are you using someone else's phone?"

"It's Doris's phone. Mine is taking forever to recharge and—oh, dear. I forgot all about calling. I'm sorry. I didn't worry you, did I?"

"No ... Well, a little. But that's all right."

"Now I feel awful."

"Mom, stop it."

"Here I am having fun and you're worried sick."

"I didn't say I was worried sick."

"You sound sick. Tired. Are you coming down with something?"

"I don't know. Maybe."

"Are you getting enough sleep?"

"No ... Nobody here does. Look, enough about me. I'm fine. What have you and Doris been up to?"

"Well, yesterday was a whirlwind. We went to her nü-metal cardio class in the morning, and then we had JG McGator's for lunch, and then we went to the pogo stick tetherball matches, and—"

"Mom! I don't want you getting on a pogo stick."

"Oh, no. We were just watching. That's for the younger crowd."

"The ones in their sixties?"

"Don't be smart."

"Sorry. It sounds like you're having a good time. But don't forget where you are."

"What do you mean?"

"Florida, Mom. ANSIS?"

"I don't want to hear about that awful disease anymore. Everything is so perfect and beautiful here. I feel like I'm in a giant, walled-in fairytale."

"There's terrible things happening on the other side of those walls."

"I don't want to talk about it, Ryan."

"Okay, all right. I'm glad you're having fun. But I'll sleep better when you're back home."

"Oh, dear ... This is so difficult for me. So, I'm going to come right out with it: I'm staying."

"Huh? For how long?"

"Forever."

"What?"

"This is where I belong. My special place. That one spot in the world where I feel totally at peace."

"You haven't even been there for forty-eight hours."

"I know. But sometimes, you just know. You know? And *I know.*"

"Mom, think for a minute. It's expensive there."

"I'm going to move in with Doris. We'll be fine."

"And you hate hot weather. If it gets into the upper seventies, you say it's *beastly* out."

"I've been very comfortable."

"You can't upend your whole life on a whim. Come home and we'll talk it through."

"I'm not going home. I'm not leaving here. *Ever.*"

"Oh? Who's going to sell your house? And pack up your things?"

"I can hire a realtor and sell the house from here. And I'll have them do an estate sale. I don't want any of that garbage anymore."

"*Garbage?* What about all your photos and scrapbooks?"

"To hell with them."

"Mom!"

"Live in the present, launch yourself on every wave, and find your eternity in each moment. That's what Al Peora says."

"Who?"

"The president of the World Village. Doris and I spoke with him at JG McGator's. He was sitting at the table right next to ours. Can you imagine? He's such an amazing man. I would do anything for him."

"Do anything ...? You just met him! What's going on? Do you have a crush on this guy?"

"No ... Don't be silly. He must be twenty years younger than me. But he's so smart. He gets you to rethink everything you've ever known, right down to your BMs."

"Huh?"

"Think about it, Ryan. Why do we call our BMs *waste?* It takes the body days to make a BM, and then we just flush it away. Most people never even look at their BMs. What are we ashamed of? A BM is beautiful, in its own way. If people can worship a dung beetle—they were sacred in ancient Egypt—then what's so bad about dung? Maybe it's sacred, too."

"*Sacred?* Mom, that's crazy! What else did this guy say to you? Did he tell you that you shouldn't go home? Did he threaten you?"

"Of course not."

"Did he make you sign anything?"

"No. Why?"

"Because I'm worried you've been scammed."

"This is *my* decision, Ryan."

"But you're not being logical. Something's not right."

"What do you mean? Not right with *me?*"

"I don't know ... Maybe. You don't sound like yourself."

"What do I sound like? A doddering old fool, I suppose."

"No. You sound like you've been brainwashed."

The line goes dead. Goddammit. I hit redial and go straight to Doris's voicemail. I try again, same result. Is Mom telling Doris not to answer?

First my PAL, now my mom.

All the women in my life are going crazy today.

CHAPTER 4

Hank's puckering and unpuckering butthole is telling him it's time to pinch a loaf, but that's not going to happen at 35,000 feet. He refuses to join the procession of mouth breathers heading in and out of the shitter. All public restrooms disgust Hank, but airplane facilities are the worst. They're tiny. They stink. And they're dirty beyond belief. Hank once read an article about a guy who conducted secret tests on the cleanliness of airline bathrooms. He found traces of fecal E. coli on the toilet seats, the flush handles, the floors, and the sinks.

The motherfucking sinks!

Hank isn't ready for that, not even after a month of Sarge's exposure therapy. It was a brutal regimen. One day, Sarge would order Hank to eat scrambled eggs off the bathroom floor (without utensils); the next, he'd make him lick the toilet seat. *(Tongue it like it's the most beautiful snatch you've ever seen, Shitley!)* The worst was the first day, cleaning up the mess from Sarge's shit sack. Hank put on two pairs of rubber gloves and wrapped the rest of his body in cellophane. But he did it. He completed every disgusting task Sarge threw at him. How could he say no? The man took a bullet for him. Now that Sarge isn't calling the shots anymore, Hank's OCD is in command again.

Hank needs to get his mind off his bowels, so he decides to give Sarge's case file another review. It's highly confidential, not something he should be looking at in public. But the old-timer sitting next to him is asleep, drooling all over his I LOVE TAKING NAPS & KILLING JAPS t-shirt, so Hank figures it's okay. The most interesting thing in the dossier, from a curiosity standpoint, is the date that the incident at the World Village occurred: October 4th. It's the same day as a mass shooting that left over a hundred people dead at TekCircle Corporation in Chicago. It would be easy enough to chalk that up to coincidence, except for the timing. According to the file, the naked girl appeared out of nowhere at the Chocolate Starfish concert at 8:15 p.m. Eastern Time, and that's the same time the bullets started flying at TekCircle. That seems like a *huge* coincidence, although Hank can't imagine how the episodes could be connected. His primary mission objective is to learn as much as he can about the girl—to make contact with her, if possible. She's reportedly being held at the World Village DUNG Center (that's Detention Under Nonmilitary Guard). Sarge has an informant in the World Village who might have a way to get Hank inside the facility. Meeting up with that person is Hank's top priority. But there's a catch: The informant's identity is unknown, even to Sarge. Hank is supposed to lay low and wait for the source to identify himself (or herself) to him with a code phrase: "The owl that flies alone is loneliest at night."

Fucking cloak and dagger bullshit.

"Ladies and gentlemen, we're about to begin our final descent into the World Village. Please make sure your seat backs and tray tables are in their full upright position. Thank you."

Once the announcement is complete, all of the window shades on the plane lower and lock themselves shut. No explanation is given for this, but it's clearly to prevent the passengers from seeing any part of Florida besides the World Village. The state is a smoldering nightmare of perversion. Fucking, fucking, and more fucking. Every sort of animal is being sodomized, from dogs and cats to dolphins and alligators. Packs of children roam the streets, looking for other kids to rape (or senior citizens or people with disabilities—anyone who's easy prey). There was even a report of a woman giving birth, shoving the newborn back into her vagina, and masturbating. Using her baby as a human dildo. As far as Hank is concerned, the whole state—including the World Village—can get swept away by a giant tsunami and rot at the bottom of the ocean.

But not just yet. He's got a job to do first.

The instant Hank steps outside the airport, he's hit with a one-two punch of overpowering heat and a vile stench. The temperature is no surprise—the average high for Florida in November is 106 degrees. But what's up with that manure-like smell? Is there a ranch or a farm nearby? It seems doubtful, given the surroundings. The baggage claim area of the airport opens onto a vast public square, on the other side of which is the World Village monorail station. The monorail is the quickest and easiest way for newcomers to get to their initial destination, which in Hank's case is his rental house.

Hank makes his way across the plaza, suitcase in hand, doing his best to ignore the stink as he takes in the sights: bubbling fountains, a 1950s-style bandstand, and flower beds exploding with color. The people milling about are mostly coffin dodgers, but there are some younger folks, too—even some kids (those under fifty-five can apply for a work visa or a visitation visa for entry into the World Village). Regardless of their age, everyone is put together just so with their collared shirts and tailored slacks, blousy tops and culottes. Toss a penny in any direction, and you'll hit a five-thousand-dollar handbag. Hank feels like an idiot in his Dick Withers crested polo shirt and tan pleated chinos. He'd be a lot more comfortable in a t-shirt and a pair of cargo shorts, but Sarge told him to blend in, so that's what he's doing. Blending in and looking like a prick.

Overshadowing everything in the plaza is a twenty-five-foot-tall statue. It shows a man, dressed in a suit and tie, with his arms outstretched in greeting. Hank reads the plaque at the base:

"I welcome you to the happiest hometown in the world."

- B. Alfred Peora

Well, well. The mysterious Mr. Peora is finally revealed. Sort of. The dark bronze makes it hard to see the statue's details, plus the face has been bombarded with bird poop. There are no known photos of Peora, and this statue does nothing to help identify him. Hank's secondary mission objective is to gather as much information about the guy as possible. The best would be to talk with him, but a chance to do that is unlikely given the elusiveness of the World Village's leader. Hank will have to see how things play out.

There's a large brick gateway up ahead, signaling the beginning of another section of the plaza. A curved sign stretches overhead from pillar to pillar:

WORLD VILLAGE SCULPTURE GARDEN

A Celebration of American Stool Production

What the hell ...? Bar stools, maybe?

It's the goddamndest thing. People in the World Village have gone coo-coo for poo-poo.

No, Hank tells himself. Impossible. But as soon as he passes through the archway and into the garden, he sees that he's wrong. *Very* wrong. The first sculpture, a few yards up the path, looks like a giant Baby Ruth candy bar. It's bigger than a bus! There's a placard in front of it:

Lumpy and Sausage-like Stool, Mild Constipation
(Medium: Plaster mold, human excrement)

The breeze shifts and blows across the sculpture. *Jesus fuck!* It's like getting a shit suppository crammed up each nostril. Hank forces back a mouthful of bile. Dread washes over him as he realizes he's standing a few feet away from a crap-covered monstrosity. And it's not the only one. The path breaks off in multiple directions, winding around dozens of other sculptures, all of them big and brown. One of them is shaped like a coil of poop with a ladder mounted to the side. Kids are climbing it and sliding down the swirl, laughing as they smear their clothes with shit.

Hank's heartbeat is a timpani cadence in his ears. It feels like he's suffocating, the sights, sounds, and smells of the sculpture garden crashing down on him from all sides. He needs to get out of here—NOW—before his fear overwhelms him. Incapacitates him. He starts to run. Hank knows he must look ridiculous, sprinting with a suitcase like a business traveler making a mad dash to catch their red-eye flight. So much for blending in. Fuck it. All that matters right now is escaping the sculpture garden. The exit is in sight. He needs to keep running ...

This place is a nightmare!

Running ...

A goddamned shitshow nightmare!

Running ...

The World Village is divided into six "worlds": Beauty, Harmony, Prosperity, Tranquility, Security, and Integrity. Each world has its own neighborhoods, restaurants, shopping malls, golf courses, amusement parks, town squares, and community centers. Traveling by monorail, residents can make a loop through all six worlds and back again. Hank is slumped in a window seat, pulse racing, still reeling from the horrors in the park. He's doing his 4-7-8 breathing exercise (inhale for four seconds, hold it for seven, exhale for eight), trying to prevent an all-out panic attack. He wasn't expecting to be assaulted by the residents' love of poop right off the bat. Even the monorail cab stinks like shit! Maybe some of those kids from the slide came on board? No ... he doesn't see any of them. What reeks then?

Maybe it's you.

Oh, great.

Maybe you brushed against one of the sculptures.

Here we go again.

Maybe there's poop on your shirt.

It's Hank's inner OCD voice. Taunting him. Trying to draw him into a bottomless pit of bad thoughts.

You should go to the washroom and change your clothes, just to be safe.

Forget it, Hank tells himself. He's not falling for this.

On second thought, the washroom is probably contaminated, too. Shit everywhere. But you can't sit there in a poopy shirt. Maybe you should strip it off right here and—

STOP!!!!! Hank *knows* he didn't touch one of those sculptures. He didn't get closer than four feet from any of them. He needs to turn off his goddamned brain. Hank looks out the monorail window to distract himself, watching the scenery glide by. Fancy entrance signs lead into neighborhoods with quaint courtyard villas and manicured lawns. Palm trees line the roadways. Luxury vehicles cruise up and down the streets, but not in the far-right diamond lanes. Those appear to be reserved for ...

Rolling porta-potties?!

Hank must not be seeing things right. Either that or he's losing his mind. Because it looks like chemical toilet stalls are zipping right along with the cars. Some of the port-o-johns are your standard aqua blue, while others have custom paint jobs. Hank spots one that's green and gold with the Green Bay Packers logo. Another one is red and decorated with the Confederate flag emblem.

Hank taps the shoulder of the man sitting in front of him. "Excuse me. Am I crazy, or am I seeing shitters on wheels down there?"

The guy turns around and smiles a mouthful of Polident-polished chompers. His eyebrows look like mutant albino caterpillars. "You must be a newbie. They're dump runners."

"Huh?"

"*Dump runners.* That's what we call our motorized latrines. They're the most popular way to get around in the World Village."

"There's people inside those things?"

The man laughs. "What did you think? That they're driving around by themselves?"

"But how ...?"

"There's a window cut into the door, so you can see the road. You sit on the toilet seat, and the engine is down in the commode."

"They're not working toilets?"

"Not unless you want to crap up your motor."

"How do you steer?"

"A handlebar unit comes up from the floor."

"I thought people drove golf carts in retirement communities."

"Yeah, we used to do that. But then President Peora souped-up a potty, and it caught on."

"Peora? That's quite a statue of him back at the airport. Have you ever met him?"

"Just once. It was my first day in the World Village. I moved down here after my darling Alice passed. I was having lunch at JG McGator's, feeling lost and alone, when who should sit at the table next to me?"

"Al Peora."

"Right-o! Well, we got to talking, and I told him I wasn't sure if I could do this. Everything seemed so overwhelming. And you know what he told me? He said I needed to live in the present, launch myself on every wave, and find my eternity in each moment. Isn't that nifty?"

"Yeah, that's ... Something."

"I'll tell you what—I'd do anything for that man."

"That's a little intense."

"You'd understand if you met him."

"I'd like to meet him. Is that possible?"

"Oh, you might run into him one day. The more you're out and about, the better your chances. You should sign up for lots of clubs and activities, like me. I'm in a tickle-fight league. I play unicycle field hockey. And I joined a coprophagia club."

"Copro-what?"

"*Coprophagia.* The consumption of feces."

Hank wrinkles his face. "Christ on a cracker."

"Now, now. Don't poo-poo eating poo-poo. Have you ever tried it?"

"No!"

"It's an acquired taste, I'll admit. Very pungent. The flavor and texture are a bit like limburger. But sweeter ... earthier."

Maybe Sarge's exposure therapy is paying some dividends after all. A month ago, hearing a revolting description like that would have made Hank puke. Now, it merely disgusts him. "You're not worried about getting sick?"

"Spoken like a true croaker stroker."

"A what?"

"Oh, that's right. You're a newbie. A croaker is a doctor. A croaker stroker is someone who buys their baloney. Croakers aren't in touch with reality, especially when it comes to excrement. Think about it for a minute. Babies receive all the nourishment they need from their mothers' milk. A man who's lost in the desert can stay hydrated and keep himself alive by drinking his own urine. Our bodies produce miracles! Except for feces? Eat some of that, and you'll die? That's crazy! If it doesn't pass the common-sense test, you know it's not true. You can't believe what you hear from the mainstream media, either. They're all in league with the croakers. The only news program I watch is *Talking Shit* with Carl Tuchus. That guy tells it like it is!"

"Never heard of him. What network is he on?"

"He's local. Channel 2. The Deuce."

The conductor pipes in over the PA system: "Now approaching Beauty Station. If Beauty is your destination, please begin making your way to the doors. Next stop, Beauty Station."

"This is where I get off," Hank says.

"It was a pleasure chatting with you."

"Wish I could say the same."

The man's big dumb smile disappears in a contemptuous huff.

Hank picks up his bag. "Catch ya later, turd breath."

As he shimmies up the aisle, Hank realizes that his urge to poo is making a sudden and uncomfortable return. Maybe it's all this shit talk that did it. Or perhaps it's the inevitability of fighting against his sphincter (you can win a battle, Hank has learned, but not the war). In any case, it doesn't feel like he's going to be able to wish away his BM this time. It's a twenty-minute cab ride from the station to his rental. There's no way he can hold out that long. He's going to have to do the unthinkable and use a public restroom.

Hank exits the monorail with a handful of other passengers and heads straight for the men's room. When he steps inside, he can't believe what he sees: It's spectacular! There are marble floors and stained-glass chandeliers, mosaic tiling and mahogany cabinets. The room smells like a mix of flowers and evergreen trees. There's even an attendant bot on duty. It looks like the Tin Man in a tuxedo.

"Hello, sir. I'm LANCE, your Lavatory Auto-Narrated Concierge Experience. How may I assist you today?"

"I think I know the ropes, LANCE."

There are four stalls, and they all appear to be unoccupied. Hank checks out the first one, and it's as immaculate as his bathroom back home. This is a potty paradise. A lavatory la-la land. Just a quick check to make sure there's plenty of toilet paper ...

Aaaaaaaaaand, no.

There's *no* toilet paper. Not even a toilet paper dispenser. He checks the second stall: Nope. And the next: Nada. And the last one: Zilch.

"Umm, LANCE? We've got a TP crisis over here."

"Toilet paper isn't permitted in the World Village, sir."

"What?"

"It's illegal to buy, sell, own, manufacture, distribute, transport, or use."

"Why in the hell ...?"

"Toilet paper hurts the environment. Its production destroys more than one hundred and fifty thousand trees a day."

"What am I supposed to wipe with?"

"Wiping is bad for you. Most people do it too long and too hard. It causes anal itching, fissures, and bleeding."

Hank gestures toward the stalls. "Are there bidets in there? I didn't see any."

"Bidets waste water. Also, repeated bidet use is unhealthy for women. It upsets the micro flora in the vagina, resulting in bacterial vaginitis as well as—"

"CRAM IT!"

Hank can't argue with this mechanical nitwit anymore. He needs a TP alternative—and fast! He scans the room for facial tissues, hand towels, or even a newspaper. Nothing. He doesn't have any of those things on him, either. All he has is his suitcase.

His suitcase.

Full of clothes.

Jesus fuck.

Five minutes later, Hank emerges from the restroom stall, his suitcase a tad lighter than when he entered. In the toilet behind him, two pairs of his crew socks are streaked with shit and soaking up water in the bowl. He walks to the sinks to wash his hands.

"Can I offer you some cologne, sir?" LANCE asks. "Breath mints? Gum?"

Hank glares at him. "Tell me one thing. Who's responsible for this ban on toilet paper?"

"President Peora, naturally. He issues all of the executive orders in the World Village."

After a thorough washing, Hank pokes the button on the hand dryer and takes a minute to lose himself in the white noise. To focus.

Secondary mission objective, my ass.

Finding Al Peora has moved up Hank's list of to-dos. He's not leaving the World Village until he has a few words with that wack job.

This assignment just got personal.

CHAPTER 5

The TekCircle cafeteria is a raucous zoo.

It's one of the workcamp's few common areas, which means that both the Men's Wing and the Women's Wing have access to it. The guys are always in rare form, working hard to show off for their curvy, latex-bound counterparts. Fights and bullying during lunch are as inevitable as the indigestion that follows. Aside from the men's room, this is my least favorite place to be at TekCircle.

I watch Keerin wolf down another mouthful of his chipped beef on toast. It's today's lunch special. Shit on a Shingle. He attacks it with gusto—reminds me of when my dog Trixie used to lap up her own diarrhea.

"I don't know, sir," Keerin says. "I don't think your mom could've been brainwashed. That's some intense stuff. It doesn't happen in a day or two."

The same thought had occurred to me. Still ... "Maybe there's an advanced technique?"

"Isn't it possible she fell in love with the place and wants to live there?"

"No. No way."

"Why?"

"It's a long story."

"I'm willing to listen."

Hmm ... Do I want to talk about this with Keerin? He's a nice enough cube-mate, but I've never really considered him a friend. I don't think of *anyone* at TekCircle as a friend. If I'm going to dredge up the past, it should be with a therapist, not an eighteen-year-old I barely know. Aw, what the hell. I guess I can give him the Cliff Notes version. "When I was thirteen, my sister died. She had just finished high school.

"Holy cow ... so young. I'm sorry. Do you mind if I ask ...?"

"She hung out with a rough crowd. They did some crazy shit, and ... I don't want to get into it."

"Hey, no worries."

"About a year later, my dad passed away."

"That sucks."

"My mom had a nervous breakdown. Her grief overwhelmed her, and she couldn't live a normal life. If something made her laugh, like if she was watching a sitcom, she'd end up crying for hours. What right did she have to feel happy, even for a moment, when her daughter and husband were dead? That's the mindset she was in."

"I'm sorry she went through that."

"I finally convinced her to see a therapist. That helped—*a lot*—but it was a long road to recovery. I had been planning to go to college out of state. Considering everything she was dealing with, I couldn't do it. So I rearranged my plans—my whole future, really—to be with her. And I'd do it again—don't get me wrong! But after making a sacrifice like that, there's no way I believe she'd be so indifferent about moving away. Somebody got into her head. I'm betting it was this Al Peora fuck."

"Why him?"

"That line he fed her. Launching yourself on every wave and all that crap? I thought it sounded familiar, so I looked it up. It's a quote from Thoreau."

"So?"

"So Peora's a phony. A con man. I couldn't even find anything about him on the internet. The World Village website lists B. Alfred Peora as president and CEO of World Village Incorporated. That's it! There's no news stories. No history about the guy. No photos. Not anywhere. Doesn't that seem strange?"

"Yeah. But it doesn't mean he's a criminal. He sounds like a genius to me."

"*What?* Why?"

"He had the foresight to put up that wall."

"But what if the ANSIS outbreak had never happened? Then what purpose would the wall serve? Think about it. Maybe the wall was designed to control the residents of the World Village. Maybe the place is nothing but a giant prison."

"What are you going to do about your mom?"

"I need to talk with her."

"Keep calling. She'll pick up eventually."

"No. I don't think so. Something's wrong. I need to see her. In person. Now."

"How's that going to happen?"

"I'm going to the World Village."

Keerin looks baffled. "*Going?* How?"

"I'll have to take some days off."

The cafeteria goes silent.

Uh-oh ... Is the pin-drop hush in response to my comment? (Days off aren't taken lightly in TekCircle's Performance360® culture. Employees are expected to work a minimum of three hundred and sixty days a year, and most people strive to be Pride365® certified, putting in a full year of uninterrupted work.) All heads are facing the front of the room, and I realize what's got everyone's attention: Frankie Strong has entered the cafeteria. He's hobbling along with his lunch tray in hand, looking for a place to sit. The guys at his usual table have stacked their laptops and briefcases on Frankie's seat, making it clear he's no longer welcome.

As Frankie makes his way past the Client Relations table, Sam Schmaltz stands and shouts at him. "If it isn't the shit eater! I hear you chowed down this morning. Here, have some more!"

Before Frankie knows what's happening, Sam loads his spoon with chipped beef, pulls it back like a catapult, and launches a sloppy projectile. The payload hits Frankie in the nose with a wet smack. He freezes in his tracks, humiliated.

"Ha! The guy always was a brown-noser," says Owen Bean from Accounting.

The cafeteria erupts in laughter, and people start shouting in unison: "Brown-noser! Brown-noser! Brown-noser!" Even the guys at the Corporate Synergies table join in. You know you're in trouble when *that* group of losers is laughing at you. They're a bunch of stitched-together freaks from various acquisitions, two employees for the price of one, keeping themselves and their careers alive with a steady diet of immunosuppressive drugs. LickSpittle (the monster formerly known as Mitch Lick and Barry Spittle) is cackling like a lunatic. Mitch and Barry were always inseparable, and now they're literally joined at the hip, one torso melding into the other. LickSpittle hops off its chair to the floor, using its four arms to scuttle toward Frankie like a crab.

"Yahhh! Get away from me!" Frankie shouts.

Two pairs of jaws snap at Frankie's ankles. He drops his tray and bolts for the exit. More laughter and shouts of "brown-noser" follow Frankie on his way out, along with volleys of chipped beef from all directions.

"Heads up," Keerin says. "Dragon Lady at three o'clock."

I look to my right: Christina Draco is coming our way. Holy shit ... what's up with her wings? They're always visible, protruding through the slits in the back of her bodysuit, but she usually tucks them against her body so you don't notice them. Now those leathery, veiny things are spread to the hilt. Must be at least six feet across from tip to tip.

"Why is she ...?"

"Maybe it's mating season," Keerin says.

"Aw, fuck."

Christina strolls up to our table like a femme fatale, making every other seductress in history seem like a frump-a-dump in comparison. "Hello, Ryan. I understand you had a hand in this."

"This?"

"The decline and fall of Frankie Strong."

"Oh, I don't know about that."

"No? I heard you made him swallow a shit sandwich."

"Well ..."

"Don't be modest, Ryan. Modesty gets you nowhere in this business. And that's exactly where your career has been heading. Nowhere. You've cruised along for years—always competent, never exceptional. I had no idea you understood the potential of bodily waste. The power it holds. It's been used in warfare throughout history, you know, going all the way back to the ancient tribesmen who smeared feces on their arrowheads. I've always been partial to weaponized urine, especially here at TekCircle. There's nothing more satisfying than pissing all over someone's work. Maybe we could team up. Your poo-poo and my pee-pee?" She leans in close. "Or, I might even let you stick *your* pee-pee in *my* poo-poo."

Out of the corner of my eye, I see Keerin fidgeting. I glance at him: It looks like he'd rather be getting a simultaneous root canal and prostate exam than listening to this conversation.

"Eyes on me!" Christina barks, demanding my attention. "Do you want to go back to my office? Are you ready to ride the dragon?"

"I'm sorry, Christina. I'm dealing with a family emergency. I need to head out of town for a few days."

She shrugs. "Give me a call when you get back, I suppose. Although I can't guarantee that I'll still be interested. Sometimes timing is everything."

Christina turns and walks away, leaving Keerin and me to watch her perfect ass and spectacular wings sashay in unison.

"I can't believe you turned her down," Keerin says. "I know you're worried about your mom. But still ..."

"I couldn't sleep with her. I've been here too long. I knew her back when she was old, before she started casting spells. Gray hair, saggy tits. In my mind, I'll always see her that way."

"Holy cow. Well, anyway, if you're serious about visiting your mom, you better put in your request right away. Days off need CEO approval."

I shake my head. "I don't have time to run it up the chain."

"So ...?"

I can't believe I'm saying this, but it's my only option. "It's time to dust off my gas mask. I'm going down to the Executive Bunker."

CHAPTER 6

"YOU GOTTA OVERNIGHT ME SOME GODDAMNED TOILET PAPER!"

Hank is at his rental house, shouting at Sarge over the phone.

"Simmer down, Shitley."

"Don't tell me to simmer down. Did you know about this no-toilet-paper business?"

"No! I barely have any intel. That's why I sent you down there. All I've got is a mole who feeds me bits and pieces of info. Speaking of ... Has my source reached out to you?"

"No. No news about owls. Just send me some TP."

"No can do."

"What's that?"

"You're supposed to be assimilating. If the locals don't use TP, *you* don't use TP. *Capiche?*"

"Listen, you son of a—"

"Hold on, hold on! Stevie wants to talk to you."

There's a rustling sound as Sarge places the phone against his stoma.

"Mr. Hank ...? Kin I ask you sumfin? If I hads one wish, I'd wish ta visit DoodyWorld. They say it's the crappiest place on earth, and that sounds really keen ta me. But Sarge says we can't go cuzza his ass-muh. He'd be wheezin' like a tea pot! So, since you's down there anyways, couldja get me one-a them Doody-World hats? Y'know ... the Crappo Chapeau. Pweeeeeeeez?"

Since wiping his ass with a handful of socks, Hank is no longer taken in by Stevie's cutie-pie charm. "Cram it, you phony little asshole!"

Stevie is silent for a moment, and then he starts bawling. "Waaaaaaaaaaaah!"

There's more rustling as Sarge takes the phone back.

"Now look what you did! You made Stevie cry. What did you go and do that for? What did the little guy ever do to you?"

"CRAM IT!"

Hank hangs up. He only called Sarge in the hopes of wrangling some toilet paper. If that's not going to happen, there's nothing to talk about.

Christ. I need a Dewar's dinner.

The house is fully furnished but not fully stocked. Hank doesn't have any wheels, either. His rental car won't be available until tomorrow, and there's *no way* he's getting a dump runner. His best option appears to be JG McGator's—he noticed one within walking distance during the ride from Beauty Station. Hank would prefer a hole-in-the-wall dive bar over some gimmicky chain restaurant, but as long as they're pouring, he supposes it will do.

Hank steps out into the steamy Florida night. It feels like it hasn't cooled off a bit since earlier that day. At least the sun is down, and there's no stink now that he's miles from the sculpture garden. As for the horrible smell on the train, Hank has deduced that it was the collective funk of a cab full of unwiped asses. *Bleah!* He's praying that JG McGator's won't be crowded.

All is quiet in Hank's neighborhood except for a chorus of katydids and the occasional bleating of a bullfrog. Most of the houses that Hank passes are dark. Is everyone in bed for the night at 8 p.m.? That doesn't jibe with the World Village's reputation as a swinger's paradise. Although who's to say what people are doing behind closed blinds. Maybe they're wearing UV goggles and having poo orgies in the dark. Hank shudders at the thought. The only thing worse than watching a turd come out of a wrinkled old ass would be to see it in the eerie green glow of night vision.

When Hank reaches the end of his subdivision, he takes a right onto the main boulevard, walking in the diamond lane. There aren't many dump runners out tonight, although a few zoom past him now and then. One of them honks at Hank, showing off a horn that's been tricked out to make fart noises.

A five-minute walk along the boulevard brings Hank to JG McGator's. The parking lot is an assortment of cars and dump runners—not many customers, thankfully. Hank makes his way inside and is accosted by a hostess wearing a green foam hat shaped like an alligator's head. She's young, early twenties.

"Chompity-chomp, sir! What are you looking to take a bite out of this evening?"

Hank isn't positive, but he thinks he's getting a whiff of shit off of her. "Scotch. I'd like a big bite of Scotch."

"Fantastic! Head on over to the Swamp!" She points to the restaurant's bar area, which is decorated to look like an old bayou shack. A fan boat sticks out of the wall, creating the illusion (somewhat) that it came crashing through the building.

Hank grabs a bar stool and has a seat. The bartender—another youngin—greets him wearing an alligator hat and a smile. His nametag says JOCKO. "Chompity-chomp, sir! What'll it be?"

"Dewar's. Neat. Double. And there's a nice tip in it for you if you don't say *chompity-chomp* anymore."

"Yes, sir!"

The bartender sets a lowball glass on Hank's coaster, raises a Dewar's bottle over his head, and pours an amber waterfall.

The second he's done, Hank picks up the drink and drains it. "Another."

"Rough day, sir?"

"Let me ask you something," Hank says as the bartender works on his refill. "Jocko, is it?"

"Yes, sir."

"What do you think about this place, Jocko?"

"JG McGator's? It's great."

"No. The World Village."

"Oh. I like it. I usually come here from October to March. The people are friendly. Good tippers. I make enough money that I can spend the rest of the year surfing."

"What about all the shit?"

"My dad was in the Army when I was growing up, so we moved around a lot. I learned that you gotta deal with some bullshit wherever you go."

"No ... I'm talking about the *shit.* I haven't even been here a day, and I've seen a garden full of stool sculptures. I talked with a guy who thinks dookie is a delicacy. And then I find out there's a ban on toilet paper. What do you think about *that?*"

"Eh, I don't care. I've never used much of it. My poops kinda slide right out. Nice and clean."

"Thanks for sharing."

"Plus, I figure President Peora knows what he's doing. He's a pretty cool dude."

"Have you met him?"

"One time. I had just started working at JG McGator's and I was kinda in a funk, being away from my girlfriend and all. Well, the Prez came up to the bar, and right away he knew something was wrong. He told me to cheer up and said I was gonna have a great time here. Said the most important thing is to live in the present, launch yourself on every wave, and find your eternity in each moment. I've never forgotten those words."

"Sounds like a helluva guy."

"Yeah, he's one of a kind. I'd do about anything for him. Hey, I'm gonna check on some of the other customers. I'll be back in a minute."

Hank doesn't think it would be wise to slam two drinks in a row, so he sips at this one and puts on his detective's thinking cap. He's talked with two people so far in the World Village, and they've both had encounters with Al Peora at JG McGator's. Maybe he should park his butt on this bar stool, all day, every day, until the guy walks in the door. Hank knows that patience can pay off. When he was on the force, some of his biggest breaks in cases came after weeks, even months, of surveillance work. If he's said it once, he's said it a thousand times: Some things take time.

Hank also finds it interesting that Peora is at the center of the World Village's fascination with fecal matter. He thought that would be nothing but a sidenote for this assignment. But Peora is the one who outlawed toilet paper. He started the dump runner craze. The sculpture garden had to have been built on his orders. What's the connection between Peora and poop? If he's involved with chaos magic, like Sarge suspects, does shit play a role in his rituals?

"Here you go, sir."

Jocko is back, sliding a shot glass in front of Hank with green liquid on the top half, brown liquid on the bottom. "What's this?"

"Shit on the Grass."

"Huh?"

"Melon liqueur over Kahlua. It's the most popular drink in the World Village. Courtesy of the babe at the end of the bar."

Hank looks to where Jocko is pointing and sees a gorgeous young blonde (twenty-five, tops) wearing a turquoise mini dress and matching pumps. His intuition tells him that's *all* she's wearing—definitely a no-underwear-kind-of-gal vibe. Normally that would be a turn-on for Hank, but with a ban on toilet paper? That tight little number of hers could be full of skid marks. Then again, she's probably not a resident, so maybe she's not following Peora's ordinance. Maybe she's using napkins or paper towels or facial tissues to wipe, like Hank plans to do.

"I guess I'll introduce myself," Hank says.

"Careful, sir. She's not looking for a date. She's looking for a daddy."

"You know her?"

"I know her type. The World Village is loaded with 'em. They come here looking to pay off their tuition, credit card bills, or whatever."

Hank knocks back the shot and takes a closer look at the girl. She's sipping an orange cocktail as she watches a kid's show on the TV above the bar. A couple of puppets are arguing with each other, and she laughs like it's the funniest thing she's ever seen. Okay, she's probably not a brain surgeon, but that's not the point of a JG McGator's hookup, is it?

"Well, the least I can do is thank her for the drink."

"Yes, sir. Good luck, sir."

Hank gets up and saunters over to the girl. "Hello there."

"Omigod! I was *sooo* hoping you'd come over here."

"Yeah?"

"Fer sure! Your ears are so big and hairy. I wanted a closer look."

Her words tip a bucket of pig's blood onto Hank's ego. He's a nice-looking guy for his age, but damn if he didn't inherit the Shatley men's ears. His father has 'em. His grandfather did, too. Ugly globs of cartilage, way too big for the head they're dangling from. And they keep getting bigger and bigger with age. Hank knows that by the time he hits seventy, those flabby pancakes will be downright grotesque. He didn't think they looked all that bad yet. Apparently he was wrong.

"Okay. I hope you've had a good laugh," he says.

"There's nothing funny to me about sexy ears. Are they waxy?"

"*What?* No!"

The girl makes a boo-boo face. "Aw, dang."

It dawns on Hank that she's not joking around. She looks like she could cry. She *really* has a thing for his ears. "Well, I mean, there's *some* wax."

Her expression lights back up. "Really? You wanna sit with me for a while? Have some drinks? Maybe let me play with your ears a little?"

The girl is a fruitcake, but after the day he's had, Hank could use the distraction. HOWEVER, there's no point in going down a sexual path if it's going to end in a pile of turds. "I hate to be so direct, but I gotta ask you something," Hank says. "This ban on TP—what are your thoughts?"

This time the girl makes a yucky face. "If you don't wipe, you're, like, retarded or something. Doo-doo is gross."

Hank smiles and pulls up a bar stool. "A girl after my own heart."

It's three hours (and fuck knows how many drinks) later, and the two of them are stumbling and laughing their way back to Hank's place. The girl's name is Biffy—naturally. Hank didn't learn a whole lot about her at JG McGator's. She's in town visiting her grandmother. Her grandmother has an ancient cat named Cole who keeps falling asleep in his food dish, and he's always jumping on Biffy's lap with his fur matted full of tuna and liver pâté. Aside from those fascinating nuggets, Biffy talked about ears. Her recurring dream of swimming in a sea of ear wax. Her fantasy of being captured by a giant who uses her as a Q-tip, shoving her as deep as he can into his ear canal. Biffy explained how in the fantasy, the giant gets himself off by doing this. It's like his ear is a huge vagina, and he knows all the right angles to work Biffy into his inner folds and have a shuddering eargasm.

She's not just a fruitcake. She's a fruitcake with extra nuts.

The sky rumbles, threatening an evening storm.

"How much farther?" Biffy asks. "I don't wanna get wet."

"We should make it. And besides, this heat ... Some rain would feel good."

"No! I don't wanna get wet. Let's hurry. C'mon!"

She sounds panicked. Women, Hank thinks. Probably worried about her hair and makeup. She grabs his hand and pulls him along faster, leading the way without knowing where they're going.

Women, women, women.

They beat the rain by seconds, the first drops falling as Hank closes the front door behind them. Now that they're safe and dry, Biffy is all smiles again. "Got anything to drink?"

"Sorry. Tap water? I haven't gone shopping yet."

She laughs and plunks herself down on the living room sofa. "Nevermind. C'mere."

Hank joins her, and she grabs his head with both hands, pulling him in for a kiss. Her tongue tastes like a piece of rock candy. Must be all those sugary cocktails she was drinking.

They make out for a few minutes, and then Biffy gives Hank a look of drunken lust. "I wanna go down on you," she tells him.

"Yeah. Go for it." Hank leans back and closes his eyes in anticipation. He smiles as Biffy nibbles on his right earlobe. He loves it when a woman starts at the top, kissing and licking her way down, down, down. As her tongue enters his ear, Hank wonders if he's going to have an eargasm like Biffy's giant. No ... it feels kind of weird, actually. Like an undulating slug. Next, she's stabbing at his ear with her tongue—in and out, in and out, in and out—like some green-as-hell fucker trying to eat pussy for the first time. By the time Biffy starts nibbling again, Hank realizes she's not going any further down. This is it. His ear is her final destination.

Okay, enough of this.

Hank opens his eyes ...

... and sees a chimpanzee standing in the front hallway.

"Jesus fuck."

Biffy is clueless, still working on his ear. "Feels good—huh, baby?"

He taps her shoulder. "Stop it. We've got trouble."

"Trouble? What do you— AIIIEEEE—"

Hank slaps a palm over Biffy's mouth, holding it there until he's sure that her scream has been suffocated. He removes his hand. "Be quiet. Don't move."

"How did that thing get in here?" she whispers.

"I don't know."

The chimp is standing on its hind legs, rocking from side to side, shifting from one splayed-toe foot to the other. It's *big*—almost five feet tall—so Hank figures it's a male. The beast has wild eyes and appears to be gripping something in his left hand. Before Hank can determine what it is, the chimp slings it at him and Biffy like a fastpitch fireballer. A blur of motion is followed by a SPLAT—and then Biffy is screaming. Hank looks at her and isn't sure what he's seeing. She has a brown

Witchiepoo nose. Its elongated tip is drooping, stretching out more and more, heading for her open mouth.

And then Hank smells it.

No ...

It's a turd. The chimp flung it across the room, hitting Biffy square in the nose. As she continues to scream, something black bursts out of her mouth like water from a firehose. Explosive bile? No, it's not liquid. It's alive, buzzing.

Flies.

Thousands of them. They keep coming and coming, and as they do, Biffy starts to disintegrate, her body crumbling to a pile of dust on the sofa. All of this insanity barely registers with Hank. He's focused on the awful taste in his mouth. It reminds him of something he's only tasted once before. Thirty years ago.

Shitley! He's got a gun!

The Brown Underground. The water balloon.

Don't just stand there, ya idiot!

Frozen in revulsion. Then and now. A piece of poo must've spattered when it hit Biffy. And Hank must've ... must've ...

(... swallowed it.)

Cicadas buzz in Hank's brain. He's fading to black. But right before he surrenders himself to oblivion, he swears he hears that fucking monkey speak.

"The owl that flies alone is loneliest at night."

CHAPTER 7

I press the bottom button on the elevator panel—the one marked "EB"—and go down, down, past the lobby, past the basement, all the way down to the sewer level. The doors open onto a rickety metal walkway that teeters over a stagnant river of brown muck. The diarrhea stew is seasoned with condoms, baby wipes, diapers, tampons, hypodermic needles, assorted junk, and huge clumps of hair. I can't imagine what the stench is like. Thank god for my gas mask! The mask is an official accessory for TekCircle's bondage uniform. Every employee is issued a mask, but they're rarely worn—only for very formal occasions, like a meeting in the Executive Bunker.

I take slow, careful steps across the walkway toward the massive blast door on the other side of the tunnel. It's unreal to imagine that back in the old days, executives were sitting ducks on the top floor of office buildings. One kamikaze window washer could've taken out an entire C-suite! But I suppose corporate warfare wasn't as vicious back then.

When I reach the bunker's entrance, a wall-mounted scanner reads my RFID chip and the steel door slides open. I step into a decontamination chamber, which is standard protocol to take care of any toxic fumes that might have piggybacked in with me. The overhead ventilation system roars into action—a few seconds is all it takes—and the chamber door opens. I enter the bunker's lobby, going from smelly sewer to Shangri-la. Each piece of tile on the floor is inlaid with thousands of diamonds. Huge marble columns reach to the ceiling, where a magnificent chandelier hangs. It's made of bronze and crystal, twenty thousand crystals in all, and rumor has it that each one is enchanted with the soul of a TekCircle employee who died on the job. I don't know if that's true, but with so many of our execs practicing magic, it wouldn't surprise me.

Miss Gates is on duty at the reception desk. She's wearing a modified version of the company bodysuit, the latex laser-cut into a see-through fishnet pattern from top to bottom. I've had a crush on her for years, and I've never even seen her face except for those radiant green eyes that shine through the thick polycarbonate lenses of her gas mask.

Scanner gun in hand, Miss Gates aims at my forehead. A holographic readout floats in the air between us:

EMPLOYEE NO. 042 66 1968

HERRO, RYAN

Miss Gates clicks a button on the side of her mask, activating her voicemitter. "How can I help you, Ryan?"

I turn on my voicemitter as well. "I need to see Mr. Lioli."

She taps her keyboard and checks a monitor. "Hmm ... I'm not seeing you on his calendar. What time is your appointment?"

"I don't have an appointment."

"Ryan ..."

"I know, I know. But I have a situation. A family matter. I need him to sign off on a leave of absence."

Miss Gates turns to face another monitor. "What's the ticket number for your request? I'll check where your approval is in the system."

"I haven't submitted a request."

"Ryan ..."

"I know. I thought he might have an opening. Or maybe you could slip me in between appointments. Please?"

Her eyes smile at me. "Let me see what I can do."

The phone rings, and Miss Gates picks up the receiver. "Yes ...? Correct. Yes, sir. Right away, sir." She hangs up. "Well, that was easy. Mr. Lioli wants to see you."

"What? Really?"

She points down a long corridor to her left. "It's the last door at the end of the hall. Good luck!"

I thank her and head down the hallway. The doors on both sides are closed and the walls are lined with portraits of creepy-looking old ghouls (TekCircle Board members, past and present). I pretend not to notice that the eyes on the portraits are following me as I walk past. It must be the other execs—hugging their office walls, looking through the peepholes, trying to see who's meeting with their boss. I reach the end of the line and discover that Lioli's door is closed, too. I don't know if I should wait or knock or go on in. There's a click, and the door opens on its own.

The instant I cross the threshold into Lioli's office, everything feels weird. I'm tingly and lightheaded. Gravity seems off-kilter, like it's pulling me forward at a 45-degree angle. It takes all my strength and concentration to stay upright as I walk to Lioli's desk. He's sitting there wearing a gas mask that's unlike anything I've ever seen before. It's topped with hunks of black metal that jut out in different directions, each with a barbed tip. There's more than a dozen of the jagged protrusions, giving the appearance of a deadly set of antlers. Cords and cables lead from connection points on the sides of the mask to a control panel on Lioli's desk, which is covered with meters, knobs, levers, and flashing lights. In addition to the control panel, the desk is adorned with burning candles, assorted skulls (human and animal), a set of daggers, a leather-bound book with a pentagram on the cover, and a statue of a demonic-looking creature sitting on a throne. What's going on? Spells are one thing, *but Satanism?* I didn't think our leadership team messed around with that. Don't tell me those SHART nutjobs are right! Could TekCircle really be involved in a global Satanic conspiracy?

"Have a seat," Lioli says. His voicemitter has a distortion effect on it, garbling his words with feedback and echoes.

The chair in front of his desk is tilted forward, suspended in place, its back legs four inches off the floor. I sit and grip the armrests to prevent myself from sliding out. Slanted toward the desk, I find myself face to face with that creepy statue. Except for the horns on its head, the demon looks more or less like a hairy, naked man. Up close, I can see that the creature isn't sitting on a throne. It's a toilet. The demon is reaching back with one hand, holding its tail to prevent it from dangling into the bowl.

"That's Belphegor," Lioli says. "The King of Waste."

"Oh ...?"

"Pay him a tribute of excrement, and Belphegor will bring you wealth and success. But you already knew that, didn't you?"

"No, not really. Why would I?"

Lioli presses a button on his desk, and a wall of monitors behind him blinks to life. I watch as my confrontation with Frankie unfolds on the time- and date-stamped screens from various camera angles.

STRAIGHT-ON SHOT: I check my face in the bathroom mirror.

OVERHEAD SHOT: Frankie sits on the toilet.

UNDERWATER SHOT: A turd inches out of Frankie's dilated anus.

WIDE SHOT: Frankie exits his stall and joins me at the sinks. We have a brief talk. I knock him to the ground with a kick that makes Bruce Lee look like a strip-mall karate reject.

"Impressive," Lioli says. "What do you train in? Kickboxing? Capoeira?"

"Well ..."

"One thing is certain: You're a natural fighter, which is exactly what our sales team needs. Too many of our agents are mired in pre-revenue mode. It's time to actionize new opportunities. We need to align our ..."

As Lioli continues to babble, I try to figure out what's going on. He seems to think I beat up Frankie on my own. It's like he doesn't know that my PAL was responsible for it. How could he not know? My PAL would've transmitted everything about the incident straight into the minds of executive management.

Chill. I'll explain later.

Oh. My. Fucking. God.

The bitch is back.

"... in order to advance our customers through their modernization journey. It's all about pivoting to boost our organizational optimization. We need to be laser-focused on ..."

I'm sorry about earlier. I got a little carried away.

A LITTLE?

"... so we can monetize alternative niches and—THERE! Right there! That's what I'm talking about!" Lioli points to a monitor that shows me yanking Frankie out of the toilet bowl by his hair, his face caked with poop. "Clearly, the power of Belphegor is not lost on you."

Great. Now Lioli thinks I'm a devil-worshipper.

Shut up and listen! We need to learn all we can from him.

"The long and the short of it is that Frankie Strong is finished. He'll be AWS by close of business today."

AWS = Assisted with Suicide. Frankie is *really* finished. TekCircle's corporate hatchet man is probably sharpening his blade.

"Effective tomorrow, you will assume Frankie's position as lead agent in the Midwest."

"What?"

"You have what it takes. It's time to get you out from behind your training podium and into the field."

"I'm flattered, Mr. Lioli. Really! But I can't take on a new position right now. I can't even swing my own duties. That's why I came to talk with you. I need to leave town for a while. Something's come up with my mother."

"Did she die?"

"No."

"Is she dying?"

"No."

"Is she infirmed?"

"No."

"Then I don't understand."

"She went to the World Village to visit a friend. I talked with her this morning. She's ... not herself."

"How so?"

"She doesn't want to come home."

"You're concerned about your mother because she wants to stay in the country's largest and most luxurious retirement community?"

"There's more to it."

"Over three hundred golf courses."

"It's complicated."

"Twenty-five theme parks."

"Please ..."

"Ten thousand restaurants."

"Let me explain."

"No, let *me* explain. You will report to Christina Draco for your new assignment tomorrow at zero five hundred hours. Understood?"

Piss on this turd!

My PAL seems to have gone rogue. There's no way she'd be talking about Lioli that way if she was still synced with the mainframe. But, as crazy as she's acting, I have to agree with her.

"I hate to say this, Mr. Lioli. But, well ... If that's my only option, then I'm going to have to resign."

The needles on Lioli's desk gauges go crazy. A vent on his mask opens, releasing steam. My vision doubles, just for a moment.

"You don't mean that," Lioli says. "You have merger fatigue. This Cybersquare integration is taking its toll on everyone. Still, now is the time to push through, not give up. I won't let you sabotage your career. I'm placing you under house arrest until you start thinking clearly again." He flips a switch. "Miss Gates?"

Through a speaker: "Yes, sir?"

"Send in the TPs."

The TekCircle Police? Seriously? I consider making a break for it, but where am I going to go? I'm so dizzy that I'm struggling to stand. As I get up, my chair floats to the ceiling like a balloon and sticks there.

Lioli's door opens to two hulking figures dressed head-to-toe in tactical body armor. One is holding a stun gun, the other a baton.

Okay, ol' buddy, ol' PAL of mine. Now would be a good time for you to take the controls again.

Turn me back into a badass brawler?

Hello?

Maybe fight our way out of here?

Hello ...?

HELLO ...?
Aw, fuck.

CHAPTER 8

Hank settles back in his recliner and takes a sip of whiskey, letting it engulf his tongue for a moment before swallowing the burn.

"Craft bourbon?" he grumbles. "More like crap bourbon."

Hank recalls a quote from Raymond Chandler: "There is no bad whiskey. There are only some whiskeys that aren't as good as others." Easy for him to say. Back in RC's day, there wasn't a boutique distillery in every city, run by hipster giraffes with their tattooed spots and neck-stretching rings. The whiskey Hank is drinking was a retirement gift from the boys at the station. It came in a fancy little bottle and cost a hundred bucks. He takes another sip.

"Christ. Like turpentine with cinnamon."

The batch was probably rapid-aged by an MIT chemist. It amazes Hank that so many people fail to understand such a simple truth: Some things take time.

Time. Hank has plenty of it now, retired at fifty-five. With his trim physique and spiky brown hair, he could pass for forty-five. But he just couldn't deal with the departmental politics anymore—the winks and secret handshakes, constantly being prodded to attend those power breakfasts with the Chief.

Gotta play ball if you wanna make lieutenant, Hank.

Cram it.

Hank isn't sure what's next for him. He doesn't plan to sit on his duff forever. But for now, he's content to enjoy some downtime in his den. It's his favorite room in the house, filled with sports memorabilia, crime-flick movie posters, and vintage bar games. With whiskey warming his belly, Hank figures that a nap is inevitable. He reclines his chair all the way and closes his eyes. A moment later, his home intercom system is chiming. It's the middle of the afternoon, so it has to be a solicitor or someone Hank doesn't want to talk to (which includes just about everyone). A voice comes through: "Hank! Are you home? It's Harold."

Hank picks up the remote and clicks the TALK button. "I don't know any Harolds. Fuck off."

"Harold Mann. From Company A."

Wha—? The Hairy Man?

Hank springs from his chair and races out of the den, down the hall, to the front door. He opens the door, and there he is: Harold Mann, aka the Hairy Man. Back in the day, Harold was the hairiest person Hank had ever encountered. When he stripped down in the barracks, he looked like a freaking Sasquatch. It appears that's still the case, although the fluff overflowing from the collar and sleeves of Harold's shirt is gray now instead of black.

"Surprised?" Harold asks.

"That's an understatement! How long has it been?"

"Thirty years."

"What the heck are you doing here?"

"That's ... kind of a long story. Mind if I come in?"

"No, no—come on."

"I'll tie Katie outside." The Hairy Man has a hairy little friend with him—a beagle on a leash.

"No, bring her in."

"Are you sure? She's not totally house-trained."

"It's fine!"

"Let me take off my shoes. We came from the dog park."

"Not necessary. Really. Get in here."

Harold acquiesces and enters. "This is a great place you have," he says, taking a look around.

"Want to see my pride and joy? Follow me." Hank leads Harold (and Katie) down the hall to his den.

"A game room?" Harold asks. "Cool. Want to play some foosball? I'll kick your butt like I used to do in the rec center."

"Sure," Hank says, ushering him in. "But first, you have to tell me what this is about. How did you even find me?"

"I run a private intelligence firm. I pulled a few strings."

"Private intelligence? Wow, look at you! I hope you're not sore about all that Hairy Man business. We used to tease you pretty good."

Harold laughs. "Everybody gets razzed in the Army. The Sarge had a goofy nickname for you, too, didn't he?"

"Did he?"

"Yeah, I think so. What was it again ...?"

Hank is drawing a blank. "I don't know."

"Oh, c'mon. Think!"

"Hmm ... *Wiseguy?* Was that it? I used to wise off to him sometimes."

"No, I don't think so. It had something to do with your name."

"Wait, I remember. *Fatley!* That's it. I had trouble keeping my weight down, so he called me Fatley instead of Shatley."

"I still don't think that's— KATIE! NO! BAD GIRL!"

At the end of her leash, Katie is squatting out a turd onto the carpet.

"JESUS FUCK!" Hank yells.

“I’m so sorry. I was afraid this was gonna happen.”

Hank tries to compose himself. “Hey, nature calls, right? It’s no big deal.”

“It isn’t?”

“I ... guess not?” Hank isn’t so sure anymore.

“I’ll clean it up. I’m sorry.”

“I’ll get you a tissue.”

Harold beats Hank to the punch, bending over and plucking the turd off the ground with his hand.

His bare, hairy hand.

Hank stares in horror, mouth agape.

“What’s wrong?” Harold asks. “You don’t look so good.” He’s acting like it’s no big deal. Standing there like a big dumb ape with a turd in his hand.

Wait ...

An ape.

With a turd in his hand.

A-ha!

Hank closes his eyes.

Keeps them shut for five seconds.

And opens them again.

He’s sitting on the sofa in his World Village rental house. That goddamned monkey is sitting next to him, one arm curled behind his head as he scratches his armpit with the other hand. He stinks like a musty dog. The chimp is wearing a bizarre-looking helmet with blinking lights and dozens of connection ports. A few of the ports are empty, but most of them have cables that are coming straight at Hank, right over his line of sight. He reaches up and touches metal. He’s wearing a helmet, too.

“All right, I’m back,” Hank says. “Get this thing off me.”

Hank is concentrating—*hard*—trying to get himself grounded again. It feels like he's woken from a dream with a super-complex backstory, the kind where you sit in bed for a while and try to sort out which parts, if any, were real.

"There wasn't a Harold Mann in my unit, was there?"

"No, I made him up. Sorry," the chimpanzee says.

Hank watches as the chimp picks at a bowl full of raisins. He wonders where he got those. There isn't any food in the house. Then the absurdity hits him. He's focused on Diddy Kong's choice of snacks rather than the fact that *a goddamned monkey is talking to him*.

"The Hairy Man thing was your Sarge's idea."

"What? The Sarge?"

"When you swallowed some of my poop— Wait, let me back up. I can't tell you how sorry I am about that."

"Cram it."

"I'm serious. I cleaned it all up, by the way. I even washed out your mouth with hydrogen peroxide. Anyway, you went into a catatonic state."

"For how long?"

"You were a zombie for over eight hours. I didn't know what to do, so I called my contact—your Sarge—and he express-droned me this mind-control gizmo." Diddy holds up the two jacked-together helmets. "He gave me some scenarios to input that he thought might ease you back."

"Yeah? And what's *your* fucking story?"

"Just your basic talking ape. Courtesy of Al Peora."

"*What?* Peora is experimenting with apes?"

"Yep. He's got an underground lab full of 'em. It's like the final stage of a survival horror game. Some real boss-level shit. Cross-breeding, radiation, hypnosis, sleep deprivation, you name it. I was lucky. They only monkied around, pardon the pun, with my brain and vocal cords. One of Peora's animal techs, a sweet lady named Betty-Jo, helped me escape."

"What's Peora up to? What's his end game?"

"No idea. He's got a lot of pots on the fire, though. Like your friend down there." Diddy points to the mound of granulated powder at Hank's feet. A bit of glittery turquoise pokes through.

Biffy.

"What was she?" Hank asks.

"Can't say, exactly. Something Peora brought to life with magical sugar rites."

"Sugar?"

Diddy licks his forefinger and pokes it into Biffy's remains. He brings a white-bespeckled fingertip to his mouth and sucks on it, smiling. "Yeah, sugar. Yummy."

"Christ." Now Hank understands why Biffy was so concerned about getting caught out in the rain.

"Peora has hundreds of these sugar babies in circulation. What was this one's hang-up?"

"Hang-up?"

"Was she fixated on your shoes? Or your hair, maybe?"

"My ears."

"Really! That's a new one. Peora makes 'em damn near perfect, but they all end up with a glitch."

"So why keep making them?"

"They're bug control. With so much shit everywhere, the World Village should be swarming with flies. But the sugar draws them in and keeps them contained. Out of sight. So everything appears nice and perfect."

It occurs to Hank that despite all the poop in the World Village Sculpture Garden, he didn't notice a single insect. It pisses him off that he missed a detail like that until now. He hates it when his OCD affects his police work. With slip-ups like that, it's just as well that he left the force. Maybe he's not even fit for this assignment.

"Sorry about your carpet," Diddy says.

For the first time since coming out of his stupor, Hank sees that the living room floor is covered with lumpy patches of black. Dead flies—they're *everywhere.*

"Figured I'd take a few off your hands," Diddy says, holding out his bowl. "Want some?"

Hank grimaces. It's a bowl full of flies, not raisins. "Get those away from me!"

Diddy shrugs. "Once the flies go inside one of Peora's sugar babies, they form a symbiotic relationship. If they're separated, the bugs and the broad are both toast."

Hank thinks this over. "So Peora is involved with gonzo science *and* chaos magic? That's a helluva combo! Where's all this happening? Where's that lab you mentioned?"

"About a half-mile below the DUNG Center."

"For real? I'm supposed to find a way into that place. Sarge said maybe you could help. I'm looking for a girl—purple mohawk, lots of tattoos."

"Betty-Jo told me about her. Top-secret stuff. She's being held in the solitary unit. It's where they put the most dangerous cases."

"She's dangerous?"

"Must be."

"Who is she? *What* is she? One of Peora's experiments?"

"I don't know. I wouldn't want to go anywhere near her, I'll tell you that much. But since that's your assignment, I can help you. The same way I escaped from that place should work to get you in."

"Great! What do I have to do?"

Diddy grabs a small plastic case from the coffee table and unzips it. He removes something that resembles an electric drill, except it's more pistol-like in its shape. The thing looks nasty, whatever the fuck it is.

"Sit back and relax," Diddy says. "This won't hurt a bit."

CHAPTER 9

The TekCircle Police smell like shit.

Not just *bad.* No ... Like a loaded diaper baking in the sun. Like day-old dingleberries. Like a smear of brown over the treads of your sneakers.

Like SHIT.

I didn't notice the stench at first, with my gas mask on. After the TPs showed up, they dragged me out of the Executive Bunker and up to the fourth-floor detention center. I felt better the further I got from Lioli's office—less woozy, able to think clearer. But when they told me to take off my mask for my intake photo—*holy fuck!* I got a rancid kick in the nose. I hurled three times before they threw me into this holding cell. The smell isn't as bad now that I'm not right up close to the TPs. But with a dozen or so of them milling around outside the cells, their odor is everywhere.

"They're golems," says the employee in the cell next to mine.

The guy's chewing at his nails like he hasn't eaten in weeks. I think I recognize him. Grant something. Swain? Swort? Swoll—that's it! Grant Swoll. Big lunkhead from Sales Support. "What?"

He points at the TPs. "All of them. Golems."

"What's a golem?"

"A monster. Made out of clay. Brought to life with magic."

"The TPs are made of clay?"

"No, something else."

"What, then?"

"You know. Your *nose* knows."

"C'mon."

"Why do you think their uniform covers every inch of their bodies? Even their faces! Don't you think it's strange they wear those face-shield helmets all the time?"

"You're saying the TekCircle Police are pieces of shit? Walking, talking pieces of shit?"

"Right."

I consider this. "Yeah, okay. I can buy that."

"Lousy shitheads."

"So, what are you in for?"

"Nothing. Not a damn thing. I'm being framed. They showed up at my cubicle first thing this morning and took my laptop. By noon I was under arrest. They said that SHART had infiltrated TekCircle. They said there's a SHART manifesto in my files."

"Is there?"

"I don't know. If there is, somebody planted it."

"Your PAL should be able to clear things up."

"My PAL confirmed their story. My PAL says I've been working on a manifesto for weeks. But it's not true!"

"Well, maybe your PAL is ..."

"Is what?"

Maybe your PAL is deranged, like mine. That's what I was about to say. But I think better of it. Nobody seems to know my PAL is malfunctioning, and that's fine with me. "Forget it. Nothing."

"Right. Nothing. What does it matter anyway? My career is over!" Grant starts pacing his cell like an animal. He shouts at the TPs. "ALL BECAUSE OF YOU SHITHEADS!"

"Watch it," I tell him. "These guys don't mess around."

"*Guys?* They're not *guys.* They're *shit.* We already covered that. Why should I hold my tongue? What have I got to lose? Come to think of it, why hold my bowels, either? I've needed to go the whole time I've been in here. Here ... Let me show you what I think of all this!"

Grant unzips the butt flap of his bodysuit, crouches low, and releases a brown swirl onto the ground. He scoops up half of it like a handful of hummus. I sure hope he's done biting his nails for a while.

He holds up his waste for the TPs to see. "Hey ... Check this out! A nephew of yours?"

"Put that down," one of the TPs tells him.

"I'll put it wherever ... I ... WANT!" With that last emphatic word, Grant hurls his shit at the TPs. Most of it spatters against the bars of his cell. He reaches down and grabs the bottom half of his turd.

Three TPs rush his cell. One of them unlocks it, and the other two unholster their guns and enter.

"Shitheads!" Grant shouts. "All of you! Shitheads!"

"Drop your weapon!"

All of a sudden, Grant looks more confused than angry. "Weapon?"

I watch as the shit in his hand fashions itself into a knife. Not just into the *shape* of one. It becomes an actual knife. I can see the overhead fluorescent lights gleaming in the blade.

The TPs unload.

I can't tell how many shots are fired. It's about five seconds of nonstop blasts. Grant jerks in place like he's having an epileptic seizure; when the TPs cease fire, he drops to the ground. Blood pours from the holes in his bodysuit.

A baton pokes me in the ribs. A TP is standing outside my cell, reaching through the bars. "Hey. You!" Another poke. "If HR asks you any questions, you saw a knife."

"I *did* see a knife."

"That's a good boy."

I don't see a knife anymore, though. Did it slide across the floor when Grant was shot? Did it change back into crap? I'm sick of all this abracadabra! I know I should feel bad for Grant, but after seeing so many employees terminated through the years, I don't feel much of anything. Does that make me a terrible person? I just want to get in touch with my mom. God knows what garbage she's learned from Al Peora today. If I spend any more time dicking around, she's going to be too indoctrinated for me to have a reasonable talk with her.

"Listen, I need to get out of here," I tell the TP.

"Shut up."

"I'll tell HR whatever you want me to say. But I really need to leave."

"I said shut up."

"Please. Isn't there anything you can do to move things along?"

"I said ..."

Here comes Mr. Baton.

"... SHUT ..."

So shiny and made out of lead.

"... THE FUCK ..."

He's not gonna poke our ribs this time.

"... UP!"

He's gonna clonk our melon instea—

"Sir? Sir ...?"

Keerin's huge Coke bottle eyes stare down at me.

"Wha ... Where am I?"

"Your cot, sir."

"The TPs ...?"

"Gone. They dropped you off hours ago."

I sit up—fast. Oh, man ... Too fast. My head is throbbing ... probably have a concussion. Doesn't matter ... this is my chance. "I gotta get out of here."

"Before you get any ideas, check your neck."

"What?"

"Your neck." Keerin puts his hands to his throat and makes a choking gesture.

I touch my neck and feel cold metal. Aw, fuck. "Shock collar?"

Keerin nods. "They said if you try to leave the building, you'll poop yourself and talk like a retard for a week."

"Goddamn it."

"I'm sorry. Your trip to Florida is off, I guess."

"Yeah."

"I'm sure your mom is fine. Like I said before, keep calling her. She's not going to stay mad forever."

"Sure."

"Do you want me to shut up and leave you alone?"

"Yeah. I think so. What time is it?"

"About eighteen hundred hours."

"Why is it so quiet?"

"Everyone is still kind of shellshocked about ... Oh, that's right. You were gone when they made the announcement. Shoot. Well ... I'm sorry to drop this on you, but ... Frankie's dead."

"Let me guess. Suicide."

"Yes, sir. They found him in the bathroom. Decapitated. With a hatchet in his hand. Why do you suppose so many of our co-workers take their lives that way? Chopping off your own head can't be easy. I don't get it."

He doesn't get it, all right. Not a clue. Hopefully he'll wise up before he's the one on the chopping block. "Wish I had the answer, kid."

"I'll get out of your hair now. I'm going to do some more work before bedtime."

I get up from my cot, sit at my desk, and check my voicemail. There's a message from my mom. THANK GOD! I press Play:

"Hello, Ryan. This is your mother. You need to stop calling, dear. I love you, but I'm not going home. The World Village is my home now. I'm having so much fun here. And the things I'm learning—oh my word! Did you know that in the original version of the Bible, Jesus fed his disciples his BMs and urine at the Last Supper? It's true! Doris said it was never bread and wine. The story has been changed through the centuries, all because of those stupid croakers! They want everyone to think BMs are horrible, but they're *not.* It makes me so mad! Anyway ... You know I'll always love you, dear, but the World Village is what's most important to me now. So please—stop calling. Goodbye, dear."

What in the ever-loving hell is going on? Everything is coming up shit today. First my PAL makes me give Frankie a BM facial. Then Christina tells me about the power of bodily waste. Then I find out our CEO worships a poop god. Not to mention that his corporate security force is a bunch of shit golems. And now my mom is part of some geriatric crap cult? I feel like I'm going— No. Not me. I feel like *the world* is going insane. I need to get to the bottom of this. I decide to start with an internet search for Belphegor, Lioli's "King of Waste." There's not a lot of info out there, but I find some wiki entries. They all say pretty much the same thing: One of the seven princes of Hell. Chief demon of the sin of sloth. Usually depicted as sitting on a toilet. Accepts offerings of excrement in return for wealth and riches. Considers human waste a delicacy. Origins trace back to the Moabite god Baal-Peor.

Baal-Peor. Why does that sound familiar?

"It's an anagram. For B. Al Peora."

I turn and look to my left. My sister Liz is sitting cross-legged on my cot.

Yeah, that's right.

My sister who died when I was a teenager.

CHAPTER 10

Materials needed to wreak havoc in the World Village:

- -1 leaf blower
- -1 paint roller
- -1 role of duct tape
- -1 extra-large gunny sack
- -100 rolls of toilet paper

The first four items were available at the hardware store. The toilet paper was another matter. Hank needed to have Sarge express it to him. (Sarge was happy to oblige so long as Hank wasn't going to wipe with it.) Now Hank is walking the paths in the World Village Sculpture Garden, shooting toilet paper in all directions. The streams of TP ripple like a gymnast's dance ribbon as they fly through the air.

The toilet-papering gun was easy enough to assemble: 1) Duct-tape the paint roller, minus the roller cover, to the end of the blower, 2) Slide on two rolls of toilet paper in place of the roller cover, and 3) Hit the power button. When the rolls are empty, Hank grabs two more from the gunny sack slung over his shoulder and repeats. He's shooting to the left and the right, aiming at the turd sculptures and draping them in TP. The residents in the park are aghast, pressing their hands against their faces in exaggerated displays of disbelief. Outside the walls of the World Village, ANSIS-infected lunatics are fucking for days on end, the congealed pus from their open sores fusing them together, turning them into writhing heaps of disease. And yet this—the toilet-papering of some ridiculous statues—*this* is what the residents find appalling. Several of them are on their phones—calling the police, no doubt. A leathery tough guy decides to take matters into his own hands, marching up the path toward Hank.

"Now look here, buster! You better knock off this nonsense if you know what's—"

Hank points the blower at him, turning him into a mummy in seconds. The guy flails onto the grass and topples headfirst into a trash can. Hank walks past the old fool and heads through the arched gateway that leads to the front of the plaza, where the statue of Al Peora looms large. As much fun as Hank had TPing those giant hunks of shit in the sculpture garden, *this* is what he's really been looking forward to. He stands in front of the statue's marble pedestal and points his gun straight up, aiming at the noontime sun that hovers over Peora's left shoulder.

And he fires away.

Toilet paper sails into the sky, billows downward, and lands all over the bronze idol. The fresh bird shit on the statue acts like paste, holding the TP in place. Hank hears sirens approaching. He checks his watch—about three minutes have passed since he began his TP spree. The only way the police could've responded quicker would've been if someone had said an Asian was causing the disturbance. By the time Hank unloads his last two rolls, five squad cars have pulled up to the plaza's entrance. Seven officers emerge from the vehicles, all dressed in riot gear, all with their guns drawn. (Maybe somebody *did* say the perp was Asian.)

"DROP YOUR WEAPON! DO IT! NOW!"

The command is ridiculous. (A leaf blower is a *weapon?*) But Hank was on the other side of this situation countless times in the FRAT, so he knows he'll be in a world of trouble if he doesn't comply. He places the blower on the ground and raises his hands.

"GET ON YOUR KNEES!"

Hank does as he's told.

"LIE DOWN! ON YOUR BELLY!"

Hank continues to follow orders.

"ARMS OUT TO YOUR SIDE! LIKE YOU'RE MAKING A MOTHERFUCKING SNOW ANGEL!"

That one is pretty funny. But Hank doesn't laugh or smile, just obeys. Then there's a knee against his spine and his arms are pulled behind his back and cuffed. The rest of the cops form a circle around Hank. *Uh-oh* ... Sometimes compliance gets you a world of trouble regardless. In an instant, all Hank can see is a blur of jackboots. Through the repeated kicks and searing pain, he takes comfort in one thing:

Everything is going according to plan.

{ESTABLISHING LINK:\ status = inProcess(); progress = [44%]/** please_wait}

Hank's jail cell appears to be standard size, about six feet by eight feet. The door is solid except for a small window that opens and closes from the outside. Hank imagines that it's used to give prisoners their meals. It's closed now, so Hank has nothing to look at except what's in his cell. There's a sink, a toilet, and a cot, and they're all tiny and made of metal. Hank is sitting on the cot, taking inventory of his injuries. His left eye is swollen shut. The agony that accompanies each breath tells him he's got a cracked rib or two. And overall, he feels a little out of it—probably concussed. He needs to make sure he stays awake and alert for another hour or so, when he'll set the next phase of the plan in motion. (The first phase was getting arrested on a serious enough charge to be brought to the DUNG Center.)

{ESTABLISHING LINK:\ status = inProcess(); progress = [45%]/** please_wait}

There's a small black panel next to the cell door like Diddy Kong said there would be. Ostensibly it's a loudspeaker, but it's also a chip reader (if an inmate should ever overpower a staff member and take them hostage in their cell, the reader gives the microchipped employee a secret means of escape). Here's how Diddy laid it out: When Hank steps up to the reader, it will identify him as Prison Psychiatrist Dr. Robert Krueger, thanks to the chip Diddy shot into Hank's noggin. There's no such employee at the DUNG Center. It's a fictitious identity that Betty-Jo, Diddy's handler, programmed into the chip. But the system won't know that, and Hank's cell will unlock. That's when the real magic will happen! If Hank runs into an employee at the facility, they won't see Hank Shatley—beaten, bruised, and bloodied—they'll see Dr. Krueger—distinguished, doctorial, and dapper. DUNG Center employees have nanite technology in their brains that gives them a collective consciousness. Hank has a nanite in his head, too. It's called a Parietal Autonomous Link, or PAL, and it was activated by his microchip. Hank's PAL is a hacked instance of the DUNG Center's hive-mind (courtesy of Betty-Jo once again), and once he's linked with the others, they'll experience shared delusions about who he is and what he looks like. This will give him carte blanche to explore the facility as Dr. Krueger.

It's one batshit crazy scheme, that's for sure! Hank isn't much of a techie, and it makes him nervous to be relying on all this cyber-nano bullshit. But it worked for Diddy! That goddamned monkey strolled right past dozens of people on his way out of the DUNG Center, and nobody said a word except, "See you tomorrow, Dr. Krueger." Hank is crossing his fingers that it will work for him, too. For now, he needs to sit tight until his PAL's link is established.

{ESTABLISHING LINK:\ status = inProcess(); progress = [46%]/** please_wait}

Hank doesn't mind waiting.

Some things take time.

The speaker panel crackles, and a voice comes through: "I'm very disappointed to find you here, Mr. Shatley."

"Hello? Who is that?"

"You don't recognize my voice? I'm hurt. It's Alfred Peora."

For real? Hank didn't see that one coming. "Where would I know your voice from?"

"From our talk yesterday."

"*Talk?* Where?"

"At JG McGator's. I thought you'd heed my warning."

"I didn't talk with you. I didn't even see you there!"

"Don't be ridiculous. Or, wait ... Maybe you're right. Maybe we didn't talk. It's getting hard to tell. Everything keeps changing. I can't keep track anymore. All because of that purple-haired whore."

"What are you talking about?"

"I don't have time to explain it to you again. Or maybe I never explained it in the first place. It doesn't matter. The girl has to be destroyed. Even just sitting in her cell, doing nothing, she's causing alternate strands to form all around us."

"Strands?"

"Never mind. It's far beyond your intellect. What's important is that no matter how those strands unfold—or tangle—you keep finding a way to meddle in my affairs. I'm sorry, Mr. Shatley, but even though you're a seemingly insignificant variable in all of this, I need to eliminate you as well."

Hank can't help but laugh. Who the fuck does this guy think he is? "Okay, Al. Whatever you say. Give it your best shot, asshole."

"Are you familiar with the Khuk Khi Kai? It's a tower-like structure in Thailand. It was built in 1893 by the occupying French forces and used as a prison. Khuk Khi Kai translates to Chicken Poop Cell."

Those words flip a switch in Hank. Here comes the fear ...

"Prisoners were kept on the ground level. Twenty feet above them, up on the roof, was a chicken coop. Like this ..."

There's a humming noise overhead. Hank looks at the high ceiling, which is slowly retracting into the wall, revealing a second perforated ceiling. Through the holes, Hank sees the strutting feet and pecking beaks of dozens of chickens. Something hits his forehead with a plop. More plops follow—brown, green, and white—all over the room. The chicken shit that had been held in place by the ceiling is raining down. Hank is under heavy fire! He scrambles for the cot and shoves his way beneath it. He barely fits, but it does provide cover from the aerial assault.

"Do you know how sick a person can get from exposure to chicken droppings? You can contract an E. coli infection, Salmonella poisoning, the avian flu—the list goes on and on. But it's the smell that will probably do you in. Some of those droppings have been in the ceiling for days. When they decompose, it releases ammonia. I bet you can detect it already, can't you? It won't be long before your eyes, nose, and throat start to burn. Prolonged exposure is fatal. It may take weeks, maybe even months. Not to worry, we'll feed you three square meals a day until you pass. I'm not sure if you'll feel like eating, though, when you're knee-deep in feces. I suppose the only advice I can give you is to try to live in the present, launch yourself on every wave, and find your eternity in each moment."

"Cram it!"

"Goodbye, Mr. Shatley."

The speaker goes silent.

Hank stays under his cot and checks his status.

{ESTABLISHING LINK:\ status = inProcess(); progress = [50%]/** please_wait}

Halfway? That's it? Maybe this is going to take longer than an hour. But Hank isn't going to be in here for weeks, like Peora thinks. He needs to keep calm and wait this out.

Wait it out? Are you out of your friggin' mind? You need to walk over to that chip reader and get the hell out of here. NOW!

Hank's inner OCD voice has returned to torment him. And his OCD is right—his chip is functional. He could exit his cell right now. But until his PAL is integrated with the DUNG Center's hivemind, anyone who spots him will see Hank as he is, not Dr. Krueger. Maybe he could slip out undetected. Or maybe if he came across someone, he could overpower them. He's pretty good with his fists. But if it didn't work, he'd end up back in his cell. The jig would be up, too—they'd know he's microchipped. They'd remove his chip, and he'd have no way to escape again.

Admit it—you have no idea how long this is going to take. You've worked with computers enough to know that these things can stall. Sometimes for days. Or weeks! That'll kill you. You've got a way out. Take it! In case you haven't processed this yet, YOU HAVE CHICKEN SHIT ON YOUR FACE!

Another voice chimes in: *Go drink a cup of fuck, you dickless faggot!*

It's the Sarge. Well, not really. It's Hank's PAL. Diddy forewarned Hank that his PAL would talk to him from time to time—giving him advice, helping him out of a jam. He said there was no way to know what persona his PAL would adopt. It could be someone real, someone imagined, a combination of various people from Hank's life, etc. Apparently, Hank's PAL feels that talking to him as the Sarge is the best way to get through to him. Hank curls into a ball under his cot and lets his two inner voices go at it.

OCD: You're no friend of Hank! Just a nanite doing an impersonation. I've been with Hank his whole life.

PAL: You've been holding him back his whole life. Filling him with fear. I may be a bug in Shitley's brain, but you're the real parasite.

OCD: *Shitley.* Listen to you. How do you think it made him feel to be called that in front of all the men?

PAL: That was to get his problem out in the open. So he could deal with it. So he could get better. You want him to stay sick.

OCD: He's sick because he doesn't like doody? That's normal.

PAL: Don't be an imbecile. It's normal to think poo is gross. It's not normal to live every day in fear of it. To retire early because of it.

OCD: Enough with the act! You don't care about Hank, and neither does the real Sarge. He's using him to get information about the purple-haired girl. Once he has what he needs, Sarge will probably put a bullet in Hank's head.

PAL: That's it. It's time to settle this like men. Let's step outside.

OCD: Are you senile? We're a couple of voices in Hank's head. How are we supposed to fight?

PAL: I'm more than a voice. I'm a PAL. I can create a cyber battle arena and give us virtual bodies. You'll have the body of an eight-year-old boy, because you're nothing but a schoolyard bully. Me, I'll be the Sarge in his prime, not an old man in a cripple-mobile. You'll be fighting the bruiser who took out a grizzly bear with a single punch to the heart. Are you ready? I can set it up in thirty seconds. How about a back alley full of weapons wrapped in barbed wire?

OCD: Wait. Hold on a minute. There's no reason to—

PAL: Put up or get lost. What's it gonna be?

Hank's inner OCD voice is silent.

No reply.

Nothing.

It's just you and me, Shitley.

"Yeah, I guess so," Hank says.

I can't guarantee that the asshole will stay away forever. But at least for now, things will be a lot easier for you.

Hank can feel his blood pressure coming down from the stratosphere. "Thanks, Sarge. Can I call you Sarge?"

You seem to have your precious heart set on it, so I suppose so. Let's see how your link to the hivemind is coming along.

{ESTABLISHING LINK:\ status = inProcess(); progress = [79%]/** please_wait}

Look at that. We'll be ready to roll in no time. Hot damn! This is gonna be fun.

Hank checks out his reflection in the washroom mirror, running a hand across his bald head. It feels as smooth as a baby's backside, even though Hank knows that his fingers are tussling their way through his gelled-up spikes. He strokes his long salt-and-pepper goatee, his palm being tickled by bristly hairs that aren't there. Hank's PAL is allowing him to see himself as Dr. Krueger, like everyone else will see him. He's wearing—no, he *appears* to be wearing—a white lab coat with a credentials badge hooked over the pocket. He takes off the badge and examines it. The laminated card says he has LEVEL 5 SECURITY CLEARANCE. It amazes Hank that his brain can be tricked like this, to see things, *touch* things, that aren't real.

"Reset," Hank tells his PAL.

The image in the mirror changes. Hank is Hank again (in his own eyes, at least). His face is fucked. His orange jumpsuit is stained with blood. His thumb and forefinger are pinched together with nothing between them; there isn't a credentials badge in his hand.

Let's get moving, Shitley! Chop-chop!

After unlocking his cell, Hank needed to make a pit stop to get the chicken poop off his face. If his inner OCD voice hadn't been banished, he probably would have spent the rest of the day in here. Washing and rewashing, checking and rechecking. Instead, he gave his face one good scrubbing, and now he's ready to go.

Hank exits the washroom and returns to the maze-like corridors of the DUNG Center's solitary unit. The cell doors are numbered, but there's no information posted about who's inside. Is Hank going to have to open the window on each door and take a look? That might seem suspicious, even for Dr. Krueger.

A guard comes walking around the corner. Even though Hank has experienced his PAL's mind control abilities for himself, he's leery if it will work on someone else. He braces himself for the guy's reaction.

"Doc! Buddy! How's it going?"

The guard is flashing a big grin, so it appears that it's all systems go. Still, Hank needs to keep the conversation as short and superficial as possible. "Good. Doing good."

The nametag on the guard's uniform says ARTHUR. Like every other prison guard Hank has ever met, Arthur is five foot nothing. A little big shot. Napoleon with a nightstick.

"Tell me something, Doc. Are you ever going to join me and the boys for one of our Friday poker games? You blow us off every time."

Incredible. Arthur not only recognizes Hank as Dr. Krueger, but he also thinks he has a relationship with him. His mind must be ultra prone to programming. "Next week," Hank says.

"You promise?"

"Cross my heart."

"All right! That'll be great. So, what brings you down to Solitary, Doc?"

"I need to conduct one final interview with our purple-haired friend."

"Really? That's news to me."

"I just got the orders from President Peora. I'm supposed to get any last info from her that I can."

"Well, be careful."

"What cell is she in again?"

Arthur tempers his smile. That question didn't sit right with him. "You ... don't know?"

"It's been a long week. Give me a break."

"But you've been in to see her at least a half-dozen times."

"JUST TELL ME THE GODDAMNED CELL NUMBER!" Back when he was doing undercover work, Hank learned that if someone questioned his identity, it was best to double down and become incensed. A single burst of outrage is more effective than an hour of well-stated reasoning. "IS THAT TOO MUCH TO FUCKING ASK?"

"She's in Four," Arthur says, looking like a whipped puppy. "Sorry, Doc."

"FUCK OFF!"

Arthur turns tail and scurries back in the direction he came from. Hank hopes he was convincing enough to have ditched the twerp for good. He follows the cell numbers through the corridors until he reaches the one marked NO. 4, and then he pauses outside the door, feeling that old dread creeping in. Hank used to hate doing door-to-doors, knocking with no idea of what was waiting for him on the other side. In this case, he has *some* idea: A girl who emerged from a glowing orb at a concert, stark naked. But who is she? A genetic experiment gone wrong? Something Peora conjured in an occult ritual? Another one of his sugar babies? And why is everyone so afraid of her? According to Peora, she's affecting reality. Is Hank going to open the door and step into an alternate universe? A cosmic void? Questioning strangers in a slumland tenement building doesn't seem so bad in comparison.

Well, here goes ...

Hank aligns his face with the cell's chip reader. There's a buzzing sound, and the door opens.

There she is, sitting cross-legged on her cot. She looks up at Hank. "Sup, dingus? The loonies running the asylum now?"

He's confused by her comment for a second, and then he remembers that she's not microchipped. She's seeing him in his orange jumpsuit and probably wonders why in the hell he's—

Shitley! He's got a gun!

Sarge's voice is yelling in his head. But it's not his PAL this time. It's those echoes of the past again. The faceoff with the Brown Underground.

Don't just stand there, ya idiot!

Wait a minute ...

I'm hit!

No.

Return fire, Shitley! Return fire!

Is it ...?

"Whatcha clockin' me for? Jeez!"

It is.

It's *her.*

It *can't* be her.

But it is.

He's had her description all along. Eighteen to twenty-three years old. Purple mohawk. Tattoos. But he never made the connection. Why would he? How could he? The connection is absurd. Impossible. But that doesn't change what's in front of him. *Who's* in front of him.

"Well ...? You gonna say something?"

Hank struggles to speak. "I ... killed you. Thirty years ago. I killed you."

CHAPTER 11

"Welcome to Wonderland!" Liz says.

My sister and I are standing in a darkened nightclub. She hasn't aged; in fact, she looks the same as the last time I saw her: Her purple mohawk. Her BURN THE SYSTEM DOWN tank top showing off two full tattoo sleeves. She's wearing scuffed military boots, and her tights are patched together with safety pins.

Strange décor surrounds us: Christmas lights weave their way through sections of fencing topped with barbed wire. Broken mannequins are tied to the exposed pipes on the walls and ceiling. A life-size automaton—part machine, part meat—performs a spasmodic dance in a go-go cage, banging its rotting little monkey head against the bars. The place is empty except for a bartender and the duo on stage. I guess you'd call them a band? A skinny-ass punk supplies the beats from behind a bank of synths, laptops, and assorted machinery. Everything is connected with tangles of cables, including *him*, wires jacked into the ports in his bare and bony chest. The female vocalist looks stunning in her black rubber bodysuit and red corset. She's a throat singer, warbling out freaky metallic noises that rattle and echo throughout the room. There's a tray of syringes in front of her, each filled with a different color of fluorescent liquid. She picks up the green one and injects it into her neck while singing, causing the sounds she's making to become even stranger—inhuman, almost unbearable. If an alien cyborg had a shrieking orgasm, it might sound something like this.

"Pretty rad to see Newborn Trash play in such a small club," Liz says.

I'm still trying to grasp that none of this is real, that I'm lying on my cot right now, eyes closed, meditating like Liz told me to do.

"C'mon. I'll buy you a drink," she says.

As we walk to the neon-lit bar, the throat singer works herself into a fever pitch. She's holding a purple syringe in one hand, yellow in the other, getting ready for a double injection.

"I can't take much more of this."

"Fine," Liz says, giving me her patented big sister eye roll. The duo on stage vanishes, along with all of their equipment. "Better? You never did like cool music."

"What'll it be?" the bartender asks. He looks like a goth version of a romance novel hunk. Long black hair. Shirtless. Draped in chains and beaded necklaces, crucifixes dangling over his abs.

"This is all for my shits n' giggles," Liz tells me. "I've never had a guest here before. Lemme see. How about ... *This?*"

"What'll it be?" the bartender asks again. The woman posing the question now is a beautiful blonde with breasts that her halter top can barely contain.

"Nice," I tell Liz. "So, how does this work? If I drink in here, do I really get drunk out there?"

"What's the diff?"

"I can't be getting tanked in the office."

Liz shakes her head. "You're such a corporate tool."

"How can you say that? You don't even know me."

"Sure I do."

"How? You've been gone for, what, thirty years? And what the hell are you? A ghost?"

Liz laughs. "I'm one scary chick, but I'm no ghost."

"What, then? I want some answers. Now!"

"Jeez. Serotonin, please," Liz says. "Get yourself a drink, and I'll do my best to explain."

I order a gin and tonic, and Liz gets a bottle of beer. We sit across from each other in a booth, with Liz sprawled across her side like she's kicking back in a sunlounger. She takes a swig and starts fiddling with the bottle's label, working a black-painted fingernail into the corner so she can give it a good peel, like she always used to do.

"Well, for starters, I'm a tulpa," Liz says.

"A what?"

"You know. A thoughtform."

"I don't have a clue what you're talking about."

"Then I guess it's time for Mysticism 101. A tulpa is, like, an imaginary friend who can think for themself. A thought brought to life with mental energy."

"Brought to life? By who?"

"In my case? You."

"Me?"

"Yeah, back when you were in high school. Liz's death hit you hard. You thought about her all the time."

"What do you mean, *her?* You're not Liz?"

"I'm Liz, but I'm not your sister. I'm a version of her that you created. I have a lot in common with her, but I'm my own person, too. Liz 2.0, you could say."

I'm trying my damnedest to follow along. "Okay ... And how, exactly, did I create you?"

"Like I said, Liz was on your mind a lot. Especially at night. When you were drifting off to sleep, you'd talk to her, ask her questions. Night after night. Finally, one night, I answered."

"I still don't get it. *How?*"

"I can't tell you all the ins and outs of how the brain works. But I do know this: Hypnagogia is a powerful state of consciousness. Like, wicked powerful!"

"Whoa! Slow down, Professor. Hypna-*what?*"

"Hypnagogia. It's when you're right in between being awake and sleeping. That's when you brought me to life. When I became the little voice in your head."

"There's a voice in my head, all right, but it's not you. It's my PAL."

"After you started working at TekCircle, you talked to me less and less. You had a lot of other stuff on your mind. I understood. I was still there if you needed me. Project Hivemind changed everything. When your PAL found me hanging out in your brain, it decided to hijack me. Turned me into a marionette with TekCircle pulling the strings. All of a sudden, I'm telling you that the cornerstone of business excellence is exceeding customer expectations. And that there's no 'I' in teamwork. I sounded like a total dingus! But you never even noticed the change, 'cause your PAL wiped me from your memory."

"That's not true! I never forgot about you, Liz."

"You never forgot about *your sister.* I'M NOT HER! I'm a thoughtform version of her. You forgot about *me.* Forgot I ever existed in your mind."

It starts coming back to me like a lost dream piecing itself together. All those late-night conversations that helped me get through so much: Liz's death. Dad's stroke. Mom's breakdown. Liz—*my* Liz, Liz 2.0, the Liz in my head—was always there for me. "Oh, man ... I did forget, didn't I?"

"Yeah, big time. Luckily, your PAL didn't have total control. Part of me broke free and hid—deep in your mind, right here in Wonderland. I built this place to chill and figure out how your PAL works. And how to override it. I gave it a dry run in the crapper with Frankie this morning. I was pretty happy with the results."

"Really? Frankie's dead."

"So? We didn't kill him."

"No, but we gave TekCircle the excuse they needed to take him out."

"PUH-leeze! That was gonna happen regardless. Besides, I'm not talking about what we did to Frankie. I took control of your PAL. I took control of *you*. And I did it all without TekCircle's hivemind knowing a damn thing. I'd call that a success, boyo."

"I suppose."

"I thought for sure you'd recognize me. I was acting like myself again. Talking like myself again. It felt good."

"I knew something was different, but ..."

"But you still didn't remember me. So I came back to Wonderland and did some more tinkering. I figured if I could make you see me, not just hear me in your head, that would do the trick."

"When you showed up in my cubicle, could anyone else see or hear you? Keerin?"

"Only you. I projected myself from your brain, kind of like a mental hologram."

"Can you exist out in the world?"

"Nope. Only in your mind."

"Are you sure? Isn't it possible? Somehow? Maybe using the power from my PAL?"

"I don't think so. Why?"

"Because Mom's in trouble, and I can't do a goddamned thing about it with a shock collar on."

"You want me to pop out of your head and catch a flight to Florida? That ain't gonna happen."

"Fuck! Why didn't you stick with me in Lioli's office? I needed you!"

"Kicking Frankie's ass was one thing. Taking on Lioli with his Satanic magic, that's something else. We weren't gonna win that fight."

"What can we do?"

"You need to play nice for a while. Convince everyone you're a company yes-man again. They gotta take off your collar sometime. When they do, we can slip out of here."

"That could take months! What happens to Mom in the meantime? She could give her life savings to Al Peora. Or should I say Baal-Peor? Nice catch on that. What kind of person names himself after a Moabite god? It's an alias, obviously. What does he have to hide? Who is he?"

"I think I know."

"You do? Who? Tell me!"

Liz stares through me. I watch the color drain from her face. My confidant, my rock, my protector, looks terrified. "Uh-oh ..."

"What's wrong?"

"We've got trouble. *Big* trouble. You gotta wake up, Ryan."

"What's going on?"

"I'm serious. You gotta wake up. Right now!" Liz grabs my gin and tonic and splashes it into my face.

I sit up in my cot—confused, disoriented.

Someone is standing next to me wearing a poop emoji mask and aiming an assault rifle at my head. A muffled voice says, "I'm sorry about this, sir."

"Keerin?"

"I wish I could spare you. I really do. You're my best friend. But SHART is bigger than friendship. A point has to be made. Loud and clear."

Aw, fuck.

This is how I die? At the hands of Keerin Shootm—

CHAPTER 12

"Your name is Elizabeth, right?" Hank asks the girl. "Elizabeth Herro?"

"Yes. And no."

Hank can't believe he's getting doublespeak from a dead girl. "C'mon!"

The girl lies back on her cot and puts her bare feet up on the wall. "It's fucklicated! Liz Herro died thirty years ago. Her brother, Ryan, made me. I'm a tulpa of Liz. Do you know what a tulpa is?"

"Yeah. A person in your head."

"Right."

"If you're a tulpa, what are you doing in a World Village prison cell?"

"Whoa ... Slow down, Barnaby Brown. Rewind. *You're* the fash who killed Liz? You're a fucking FRAT boy?"

Hank tries to calm himself down and gather his thoughts. "I used to be. Liz was in a group called the Brown Underground. We raided one of their performances and—"

"I know what happened. Bullets started flying. And Liz ended up dead. Fuck you very much."

"Hey, my sergeant was paralyzed! Those idiots fired first. I fired back and took out the shooter. One of my rounds hit Liz."

"Oopsie-poopsie, am I right? Shit happens? Doubt you lost much sleep over it. But Ryan was crushed. He brought me to life with his grief."

"Brought you to life. *In his head.* So, again—what are you doing here?"

"Why should I tell you anything?"

"Please. Help me understand. It's important."

Liz lets out a heavy exhale and shakes her head. "Jeez ... Fine. Ryan was killed about a month ago. You probably heard about it. The bloodbath at TekCircle."

"That SHART guy killed him? Fuck. But how did that ...?"

"I think it's because of how Ryan died. Real sudden. Real violent. There's an explosion of energy when that kinda thing happens. Like, ka-bloomy! That's how ghosts get made. But there was something more. Ryan's brain was full of nano."

"A PAL?"

"Yeah. How did you—?"

"I have one, too."

"You?"

"Long story. So ... You think Ryan's PAL amped up the energy released when he died?"

"Yep."

"And you were blasted out of his head? Into the world?"

"Yep, and yep again."

"I don't know how that's possible, but let's assume it is. Why did you end up here?"

"Ryan and I were talking about the World Village. Right before he died. His mom Emma is here. He was worried about her."

"So you willed yourself here? Somehow?"

"I think so. I was a total zombie at first. Didn't even know where I was. Or who. But then I snapped out of it."

"You were arrested. And brought to the DUNG Center. Why have they kept you here for a month? I keep hearing that you're dangerous. Are you?"

"Do I look dangerous?"

"No. But you shouldn't exist. Not outside of Ryan's head. You're here because of some kind of— I don't even know what to call it. A virtually enhanced sonic boom, I guess. What are the effects of that? Peora thinks you're altering reality. Maybe you are. He says he had a talk with me that never happened. But it's weird ... I can almost kind of remember it. Like it was from another life."

"So the world is changing because of me?"

"That's what Peora says."

"Peora's an evil shitface."

"What do you know about him?"

"You wouldn't believe me."

"I'm talking to a tulpa, so try me."

"Okay ... He's a demon. Like, a real demon. From Hell. Called Belphegor. He gets his power from poop."

Hank's mind is jumbled with everything he's seen and heard about since arriving in the World Village. Stool sculptures. Children playing with shit. Dump runners. A coprophagia club. The ban on toilet paper. Shit on the Grass cocktails. And on and on and on. "Actually ... That makes a lot of sense."

"The CEO of TekCircle worships Belphegor. I think a lot of your suit-types do. They spend their lives kissing ass. Why not kiss what comes out of it, too? But I don't think the office turds were enough for ol' Belphey, so he adopted his Al Peora identity and built the World Village. A fenced-in world of shit."

"If that's what gives him his power, he must be getting pretty damn strong. What does he want?"

"Beats me. I don't have all the answers. Matter of fact, I've got a fuck of a lot of questions. Like why is a FRAT boy flunky standing in my cell, wearing an orange jumper, asking *me* a fuck of a lot of questions?

Before Hank can answer, the cell door opens. Arthur stomps in with his gun pointed at Hank. He knows something's up, Hanks thinks. He knows there's no way Dr. Krueger would have forgotten the girl's cell number.

"Nobody talks to me like that!" The guard's eyes are red, like he's been crying. "Nobody!"

He fires his weapon.

Hank knows he's been hit by the impact that knocks him a step back. He doesn't feel any pain, though. No, wait ... Here it comes. *Oh boy* ... A horrible burning sensation, like a red-hot skewer is being shoved deeper and deeper into his chest. Hank staggers back another step and collapses onto the cot.

"You think your PhD makes you better than me?" Arthur shouts. "Do you?" It looks like he's getting ready to shoot again.

Liz jumps to her feet, balls her hands, and holds them out in front of her with a shout of "INAZUMA!" Two bolts of lightning explode from her fists and blast the guard in the chest. He's thrown against the wall with tremendous force, knocking him unconscious. His body drops to the ground in a heap, smoking like an overcooked slab of meat.

"Nice shot," Hank says.

Liz turns to face him. "I don't know how I did that." For the first time since Hank entered her cell, there isn't a trace of smartassness in her voice. "I remember that move from a video game Ryan used to play. But I don't know how ..."

It hurts to talk, but what Hank has to tell Liz is important. "Listen to me. I'm betting you can do ... hell, anything. You came to the World Village by thinking about it. It's time for you to find out how powerful you really are."

"What if Peora's right? What if things *are* changing because of me?"

"So what? Let 'em change. Rewrite the fucking story. Maybe there's a version where I have a better ending."

Liz looks concerned. "Ending?"

Hank glances at his chest wound; blood is bubbling from it. "I'm in bad shape. Get me pee-wee's gun."

"Huh?"

He points to Arthur's piece on the floor. "The gun ... C'mon ... The gun!"

She retrieves it and hands it to him. It's one of those vintage-style revolvers that's all the rage, designed to look like a Colt Python but modified to take modern ammo. Hank snaps open the cylinder—it's loaded with NitroJet-x rounds, which explains why his chest continues to burn like a Napalm crater. Five bullets remain. "I'll take care of the next four assholes that come in here," Hank says. "Then I'll take care of myself. You get out of here. Go help Ryan's mother."

"But ..."

"GO!"

"All right. Jeez!"

Liz steps away from Hank. She closes her eyes and takes several deep breaths. Loosens her neck and shoulders. She appears to be meditating.

"Think it and make it happen," Hank says.

She continues to inhale and exhale deeply. Again and again. After a few moments, an orange glow begins to radiate around her.

"That's it. Think it and make it happen. Think it and—"

"Shut ... up ... dingus." Liz's words come slowly, calmly. From a place of Zen. Her eyes remain closed. The orange glow intensifies.

Expands.

Envelops her in a sun-like sphere.

In a flashbang instant, the orb is gone.

And so is Liz.

Just you and me again, Shitley.

"Yeah."

Somebody has to be coming soon, with all the ruckus in here. Want some company while you wait?

"Sure."

Heh. Pretty ironic. Everything would've gone off perfect if you hadn't raised your voice with that runt of a guard. Done in by hurt feelings. Figures.

"I can beat that for irony. Try this: My OCD was right. The real Sarge probably doesn't give two fucks about me. And yet here I am, being comforted by his voice."

I don't know about that. I'm a construct of your feelings about the Sarge. Deep down, you must think he's an okay guy.

"I guess."

Heh.

"What?"

Nothing. Heh.

"C'mon. What's so funny?"

I'm wondering ... When you shuffle off this mortal coil, will you be one of the thirty percenters who blast their underpants?

"Christ."

I know. It's gross. But wouldn't that be the ultimate irony? Spending your whole life avoiding poop, only to end up sitting in a pile of it?

"Wait. Listen ..."

Footfalls from the corridor. It sounds like the clamor of several pairs of boots running toward Hank's cell.

All right, Shitley. This is it. You've got all of eternity to sort out your poop issues. Right now, it's time to aim low and kill us some more Napoleons. Hooah!

PART 2: DIFFLUENCE

A man dies and finds himself in Hell. He's greeted by a demon who says he'll give the man his choice of three rooms to spend the rest of eternity. The man follows the demon to a hallway with three doors. The demon opens the first door and reveals a room full of people standing on their heads on a brick floor. "That doesn't look very comfortable," the man says. "Let me take a look at the next room." The demon takes him to the second door and opens it. The room is filled with people standing on their heads on a wooden floor. "That's a little better than the first room but not great," the man says. "I better check out the last room." The demon takes him to the third door and opens it. The people inside are knee-deep in shit. But they're all drinking coffee as they stand there. The man says, "The smell is awful, but I really enjoy coffee. I'm going with this room." The demon ushers him in and closes the door behind him. The man makes his way to the coffee table and pours himself a cup. After he takes his first sip, the demon in charge of the room shouts, "Okay, everyone! Coffee break is over! Back on

your heads!"
-- Classic joke

CHAPTER 13

Liz is halfway up the walk to Doris's front door when it hits her. That feeling. Those questions.

Who am I? Where am I? What am I doing here?

She looks at the cosmetics bag in her hand. Turns around and sees her pink Cadillac in the driveway. And just like that, it's over. Everything comes back to her. She runs through the particulars to cement them in her brain.

I'm Liz Herro. I'm forty-eight years old. I'm a senior sales director with Mary Kay. I'm the number-one rep in the World Village. I'm meeting with Doris Akin, my new client.

Despite her affirmations, Liz is rattled. These momentary bouts of amnesia are scaring the hell out of her. Did she have a mini-stroke recently and not realize it? Does she have a brain tumor? Even though the doctors in Florida are awful, she had better get herself checked out. But right now, she needs to pull herself together and get on with her meet-and-greet.

Liz rings the front bell on the ranch-style house, and a white-haired woman opens the door. She's wearing a sweatshirt that says I LOVE ALL CATS (EXCEPT ORIENTALS). "Hi. Are you Doris?" Liz asks.

"Yes."

"I'm Liz Herro with Mary Kay. We spoke on the phone?"

"Oh, yes. Come in!"

Liz steps into the foyer with Doris. In the adjacent room, another white-haired woman is sitting on the sofa.

"This is my housemate, Emma," Doris says.

Liz stares at Emma. Something about the woman's smile makes Liz want to shove her fist down the old hag's throat.

"How's this for a coincidence?" Doris says. "Emma's last name is Herro, too."

"Maybe we're long-lost relatives," Emma says.

Doris laughs.

From a million miles away, Liz hears herself say, "Yeah ... Maybe ..." She's dizzy with rage. She wishes she could sprout talons and rip herself open. She wants to show Emma the dead boy who lives inside of her. (His name is Stevie, and he's beautiful and blue. Blue like a bruise. Blue as a breast vein.) If Emma could only see him, then the stupid cow might understand.

"Are you okay?" Emma asks.

"Yes, I'm fine," Liz says. And she is. Whatever she was feeling has passed. She's herself again. "Why don't we all have a seat so I can tell you about some great Mary Kay products, made right here in the USA, that are going to put a whole new spin on your beauty routine."

"This way," Doris says, taking Liz into the sitting room with Emma.

All is right in Liz's world.

Everything is just as it should be.

CHAPTER 14

Milk, milk, lemonade. Round the corner fudge is made.

I remember when that was nothing but a silly schoolyard rhyme. Before it became our state motto. Before the Change.

People don't talk much about the Change. Most don't even realize it happened. Some of my friends used to know about it, but now they're oblivious. That's why I keep taking these notes, so I have a record. The problem is that a lot of my notes have Changed. I looked back at some old notes the other day, and they're drawings of dogshit now. At least my memories are intact. So many memories, so much minutia. But that's okay. That's what's Changed the most—the little things. Like fire hydrants (they never used to be connected to sewer pipes). Or billboards. I can remember when billboards used to advertise things. Cars, restaurants, new movies, stuff like that. Now they're— Jesus ... I don't know. I saw a new one today. It showed a naked black man lying on his back, with his legs contorted behind his head. At a glance, it looked like he had two dicks. Then I realized that only one of the giant logs—the one he was sucking on—was a penis. The other one was a turd that he was shitting out. The billboard had one line of copy: SEVENWORM WANTS TO GO TO HELL. What does that even mean? I'll probably lie awake tonight thinking about it, and yet millions of people drive past billboards like that every day and never even notice them.

Then there's the Changes that everyone notices, except they don't realize anything is different than it used to be. Oral defecation is a good example. You'd be hard-pressed to find someone who'd deny that people poop from their mouths. It's a fact of life—sometimes it comes out one end, sometimes the other. But it hasn't always been that way. I'm sure of it because I remember a human anatomy lecture from college. We were learning about the digestive system, and the professor said it's impossible for a well-formed stool to exit the upper end of the colon. Back then, the closest thing was a condition called fecal vomiting, but that's really a misnomer because the vomit doesn't contain poop, just liquid from the small intestine. It's still disgusting, but it's not the same as coughing up a turd. That simply did not use to happen. It scares the hell out of me to think that, somehow, our entire physiology Changed. I'm not positive, but I think that America's topography has Changed, too. For instance, I don't think the Duad used to exist. Or there was something different about it—like, maybe it was a regular river instead of a river of shit. It seems like it had a different name, too. Something longer. With a lot of S's. I asked a former neighbor of mine, Jake, a while back to see if I could jog his memory.

"Nope, it's always been the Duad," he told me. "If you think that poo's rad, then swim in the Duad. That's what we used to say in grade school."

Jake was an alpha male, a hunter, and a survivalist. Not a thinker. It didn't surprise me that he couldn't remember. All he cared about was his shit guns. Like most doomsday preppers, Jake could make a fully functional firearm from nothing but shit and sticks. He loved building shit guns. Shooting shit guns. Talking about shit guns. Going to shit gun conventions. Reading shit gun magazines. Marching in shit gun rallies.

Was America always this obsessed with shit guns? Or is this another Change?

Jake was as gung-ho as you could get. He even made his own bullets. As long as your stool is hard enough, it'll work. A lifetime supply of unlimited ammo, that was his goal. He put himself on a low-fiber diet that included lots of processed and fried foods, dairy, red meat, and underripe bananas.

He died last month of complications from constipation.

All that prepping, and that's how he ended up. Dead on the toilet. Sometimes I wonder ... Maybe doomsday came, and Jake never even noticed it.

Maybe nobody did.

1968:

Henry stared at the red-haired boy in the next yard as though he was the most fascinating thing in the world. The boy was shirtless, his pink and freckled skin glazed with sweat. He sat cross-legged atop a picnic table as he poured the last crumbles of a box of Cracker Jacks into his mouth.

"His name is Freddy," Henry's mom said, standing up from her gardening for a stretch. "Freddy Peora. Why don't you go over and meet him?"

"Really?" Henry's eyes were wide with the hope of finding a playmate.

"Sure."

"What do I say?"

"Say, 'Hi, my name is Henry.'"

"Okay. That's easy!"

"Honey, just so you know, Freddy is a couple of years older than you. He's seven, I think. He might not want to play."

"How can I *make* him want to?"

"You can't. All you can do is be yourself."

"Who else would I be?"

Henry's mom laughed as she kneeled back down among her vegetables. "Good point, kiddo. Okay, off you go. Invite him over for some lemonade if you want to."

Henry ran across the sprinkler-wet lawn. By the time he reached Freddy's yard, his bare feet were coated with a thick layer of grass clippings. The moment Henry crossed the lot line, the grass felt different—scratchier, pricklier—under his feet. There were lots of brown patches, too, where there was nothing but dirt and weeds. None of that mattered to Henry, though. He kept running and running until he was almost to Freddy—and that's when his foot slid out from under him. The next thing he knew, he was flat on his back, staring at the afternoon sun.

"What a klutz."

Henry sat up. From his perch on the picnic table, Freddy was sneering at him. Hoping to impress Freddy with a quick recovery, Henry jumped up and said, "Hi, my name is Henry."

"You stink like shit."

Henry gasped. "You said a bad word."

"I don't care. Least I didn't step in a turd."

Henry checked his foot and saw that his sole was streaked brown. He was so excited to talk with Freddy that he forgot all about the bulldog that was always waddling around the Peoras' yard and making poops. "Aww ... Gross."

"Yeah, you're gross," Freddy said.

Henry wasn't sure if Freddy was kidding around or not. He tried to play along: "Oh yeah? You're gross, too!"

Freddy pushed himself off the picnic table and stepped up to Henry. "*What* did you say?"

The creases in Freddy's forehead reminded Henry of the look on Dad's face when he talked to Mom super loud about something. Freddy was mad—*for real*. Henry decided he'd talk about something else (sometimes that worked for Mom, when Dad had his crease-face on). "My family moved in next door," he said.

"So what?"

Henry thought for a second and tried again: "I like dinosaurs. Tyrannosaurus Rex is the best. He's king of the dinosaurs."

"Dinosaurs are for dorks. I'm into cops and robbers."

"My dad is a cop!"

"The bad guys are the best. My dad says all cops are bastards."

Henry didn't like that Freddy was using bad words again. He wasn't sure what to do or say. He tried one last thing: "Do you wanna come over to my house for some lemonade?"

"Milk, milk, lemonade," Freddy said. "Round the corner fudge is made." He bent over, ran a finger through the skid mark in the grass, and held a smelly glob in front of Henry's face. "Want some fudge?"

Henry turned his head.

Freddy shoved his finger closer, right under Henry's nose. "C'mon. Have some."

"Quit it!" Without thinking, Henry slapped Freddy's hand away. Once he realized what he had done, he was sure he was going to get punched. But Freddy just laughed.

"What's the big deal? It's good for you. Like spinach for Popeye." Freddy stuck his dirty finger in his mouth and sucked it clean. "Yum."

Henry felt like he was going to be sick, but before he could hurl, Freddy's hands were wrapped around his throat, squeezing with a monster's grip. Freddy's eyes rolled over red and spit out glowing embers.

"I'm going to strangle the life from you," Freddy said with a growl. He didn't sound like Freddy anymore. "I'm going to kill you before you ever manage to fuck things up!"

Henry didn't know what Freddy was talking about. All he knew was that he couldn't breathe. Was he going to die? He noticed some poop on his hand from when he slapped at Freddy. Somehow the poop made Freddy strong. Could it work for him, too? He brought his hand to his mouth and licked it.

"NO!" Freddy shouted. He tightened his chokehold.

Henry's eyes became pools of white fire, and his right arm morphed into a flaming sword. He swiped an arc of fire across Freddy's throat, decapitating him and cauterizing the gaping hole in his neck in one swift motion.

"Take that, shit-for-brains," Henry said with a blister-ice voice.

Freddy's head sailed through the air, all the way into Henry's yard, where it landed in the turtle-shaped sandbox next to his mom's vegetable garden. The head rolled several times, filling Freddy's dead-open eyes with sand, before crashing against Henry's Tonka dump truck. The noise startled Henry's mom, who turned from her gardening to look at the sandbox.

Her screams could be heard in the farthest ends of the neighborhood.

CI: Okay, next question. What's your earliest memory of a bad experience involving excrement?

HS: Let's see ... I was four. My mom played the DumDum poop prank on me.

CI: What's that?

HS: It was this stupid social media challenge. You can go on DumDum and see thousands of examples. You sit on the toilet like you're taking a dump, and you smear some chocolate pudding on your hand. Then you call out to one of your kids to bring you a roll of toilet paper. When they come and give it to you, you reach for it and get some of the pudding on them. You say, "Oh no! I got poop on you." And then you film their reaction. Some kids laugh. Others cry. Some stare in disbelief.

CI: What did you do?

HS: Good god. It was a hell of a production. First I puked. Everywhere. All over my mom. All over the floor. All over myself. Then I started screaming like I was gonna die. I ran out of the bathroom and started smashing and toppling things in the house. Lamps, vases, our TV. I have no idea why. When my mom caught up to me, I was in the kitchen, washing my hands with hot water. Scalding hot. I ended up in the hospital with third-degree burns.

CI: What do you think prompted your mom to play that prank on you?

HS: I don't know.

CI: Was it done out of malice?

HS: Nah. I don't think so. She thought it would be funny. That's all.

CI: Do you blame her for sending you down a path of coprophobia?

HS: Shit eating? I'm not into that! Christ!

CI: No, that's copro*phagia*. Copro*phobia* is a fear of or aversion to feces.

HS: Oh. That's just how my brain works. My mom wasn't responsible. Besides, after my mom's prank, nothing happened for a year or so. Then there was another episode. We had just moved into a new house, and I went to meet the kid next door. This kid was seven going on seventeen, so my only chance of making friends with him was if I really showed him something. Well, I showed him something, all right. I slipped in a dog turd, right in front of him. My foot was covered with shit, and I freaked out again. Kicking and screaming and crying in the grass.

CI: For the record, what was the name of the neighbor boy?

HS: His name was Dan. Dan Burns.

CHAPTER 15

{ARCHIVE:\->KnowledgeTransferId=<rip_plan_for_tekcircle__s+m_-_update_17>/*(restrictedAccess//Invoke)*/;
>>>_run_}

TO:TekCircle Executive Management

FROM:TekCircle Rightsizing Committee

SUBJECT:RIP Plan for TekCircle S&M – Update 17

Keerin Shootman's programming is proceeding according to schedule. He continues to be highly susceptible to the subliminal messages of his Parietal Autonomous Link (PAL), and he has begun purchasing guns and ammunition in anticipation of the Oct. 4 Reduction in Personnel (RIP) within TekCircle Sales & Marketing. He has also been keeping a journal, which will serve to document his culpability. Best of all, his brain's data transmissions indicate that he is unaware of any of his above-mentioned activities. He is proving to be quite the perfect patsy.

As we move toward the Oct. 4 execution date, please be aware of the following ongoing actions:

- We have selected seven employees from across the company to program concurrently with Keerin. Their PALs will instruct them to leave a data trail proclaiming their allegiance to Satan-Haters Against RFID Technology (SHART). This will add credence to the notion that Keerin's actions are part of a larger SHART conspiracy.

- All job postings for positions within TekCircle Sales & Marketing have been removed from the company's internet and intranet sites.

- A freeze on discretionary spending has been instituted within TekCircle Sales & Marketing.

- Managers within TekCircle Sales & Marketing have been advised to ask their personnel to compile as much training documentation as possible over the next 30 days.

- In the unlikely event that a member of TekCircle Sales & Marketing asks for a leave of absence on Oct. 4, executive management should deny all such requests. It is imperative that we have as many target employees in the office as possible so we can meet our footprint reduction goal.

- Managers within Cybersquare Global Marketing/Direct Sales have been advised to bring their people up to speed with TekCircle's Performance360® and Pride365® initiatives. These Cybersquare employees will soon have twice as much work on their plates, and their continued productivity will depend upon their acceptance of our always-on culture.

- We have begun taking bids for the construction of a larger chandelier in the lobby of the Executive Bunker.

Finally, the Rightsizing Committee is recommending that all future communications about October's RIP be carried out in code. Our update memos are not a concern because they are transmitted into the minds of executive management using restrictive access protocols. However, written or verbal conversations represent a danger to the success of our operation. Effective immediately, the RIP initiative for TekCircle Sales & Marketing will be known as Project POOP (Purging Our Own People). The committee is currently developing a series of complementary code words. Some of these include:

Mr. Poopypants = Keerin

Laxatives (and related words) = Keerin's Programming

Defecate (and related words) = Kill

Turds (and related words) = Targeted Employees

Down the Crapper (and related words) = Employee Deaths

For example:

-Is Mr. Poopypants ready to take a shit? (Is Keerin ready to begin his shooting spree?)

-No. We recommend two more days of Ex-Lax. (He needs two more days of programming.)

Or:

-Did all of Mr. Poopypants' turds go down the crapper? (Did Keerin kill everyone in S&M?)

-No. Five turds landed on the floor. (Five employees escaped the shooting.)

We will get back to executive management within seven days with a complete list of code words for Project POOP. If you have any questions in the meantime, please reach out to Barbara Blade in HR.

Thank you.

"There's a special place in Hell for mass shooters."

Scenes from the LIMBO-MS1 concourse: Piles of withered turds rot in dark and empty corridors. A headless robot sputters out sparks as it staggers beneath buzzing fluorescents. Packs of herpes-infected monkeys hurdle over broken turnstiles. An alligator devours a toddler in a puddle of hydraulic fluid.

Keerin is alone, as usual, sitting on the cement floor among the smashed remains of a wheelchair demolition derby. There are never many people around here—most of these mass shootings are cut-and-dry. Keerin is an exception because he was programmed to do what he did. Still, the chief inquisitor is arguing that Keerin was aware of his actions on some level, enough to punch his ticket for a one-way trip to Hell. His case will probably be tied up here for an eternity.

A human embryo the size of a holiday turkey drops down beside Keerin. It's strung up with wires like a marionette and sports a top hat on its lumpy, misshapen head. Keerin follows the wires with his eyes, all the way up to the catwalk at the ceiling, where he can barely make out the figure pulling the strings in the shadows.

"The guy's an asshole," the embryo says, giving Keerin a dead-eyed seahorse stare. "When he jacks off, it's like I'm riding the goddamned Slingshot at the carnival. You know what I mean?"

"Not really."

"No? Well ... Forget it, then."

A steel service door rolls up to announce the entrance of a couple of teenagers, one very tall, the other shorter, both wearing black dusters over tactical gear. They're holding guns Keerin doesn't recognize—big, bulky things that are sizzling with charged-up power. The duo walks right by Keerin and the embryo without acknowledging them. Once they're a few yards past, they break out in a fit of schoolboy giggles.

"Was that ...?" Keerin asks.

"Eric Harris and Dylan Klebold," the embryo replies. "The Columbine killers."

"What are *they* doing here?"

"Their case is more complicated than you might think. Between their shooting spree at the high school and their fiasco at the World Trade Center, they killed two hundred and forty-four people. But in doing so, they probably saved the lives of thousands."

"Huh?"

"In the 1990s, an Islamic terrorist named Osama bin Laden was plotting a major attack on U.S. soil. He was going to use planes as weapons to hit a number of targets, including the White House, the Pentagon, and the U.S. Capitol building. But his number-one target was the World Trade Center. He was obsessed with bringing it down. When Harris and Klebold crashed their escape plane into it, it devastated him. He felt like a couple of teenagers had stolen his thunder. He was so distraught that he killed himself a few weeks later. His whole organization, Al-Qaeda, fizzled out after that. Who knows what kind of damage he might have done if that hadn't happened. He was planning to use commercial jets, not a little runabout like Harris and Klebold. We ran an alternate reality simulation that ended with almost three thousand deaths."

"Holy cow."

"So we let them hang out and do some clean-up work for us."

"Clean-up?"

"Sometimes, a lesser power slips in here. They hunt 'em down. It's funny—their favorite video game was *Doom*, and now they're living out a real-life version of it, running around and blasting demons."

The two kids stop and look back at Keerin and his fetal companion. The shorter teen, Harris, shouts at them: "Stupid fags!"

They turn around and continue on their way.

CHAPTER 16

Let's get one thing straight: Joey Cologne ain't no homo. He likes muscle cars and contact sports. A real man's man. Not a gay boner in his body. Never you mind that he's eyein' up his buddy Randy's ass. They're on patrol with Randy walkin' point and Joey bringin' up the rear, so he can't help but catch a peek now an' again. 'Course, he's doin' a lot more'n peekin'. He's thinkin' how he'd like to go balls deep in Randy's pooper. But that ain't Joey! That's the Sis talkin'. Gets so bad a guy can't hardly think straight.

Joey's FRAT was sent into Florida when the Sis first broke out, to try an' calm them crazy fuckers down. Their sarge visited a whorehouse in Opa-locka, and next thing you know, the whole FRAT went down. Sarge raped Chuck, and Chuck raped Brad, and Brad raped Tony, and right on down the line. Joey and Randy is the only ones left. They was raped, too, but they ain't turned into zombies yet. They're horny as hell, though, so they come up with a way to keep their hands off one 'nother. They trapped themselves a skunk, see, and they both get sprayed each mornin'. A good poke with a pokin' stick is all it takes. Leaves 'em smellin' like rotten eggs, which don't zackly put 'em in the mood fer love. But the smell wears off, 'ventually, and Joey is prob'ly gettin' a big ol' whiffa Randy's man ass right 'bout now. Poor bastard.

Joey and Randy is doin' a door-to-door sweep of the Happy Court Mobile Homes. Place looks to be deserted, but they're checkin' just in case there's someone left to rape. That's the Sis talkin', too, but it ain't no diff'rent than it's ever been, really. Take Joey, fer example. When he was in school, he could tell if a girl didn't wanna kiss him at the end of a date. But he always got his kiss. *Always.* Just grabbed 'em and planted one—a *deep* one, too. Didn't even ask. What's she gonna do? Go cryin' home to Daddy that a boy kissed her g'night? You take what you want in this world—or whatever you can get, at least. Just gotta figure out the best way to do it. By the time he was a soft-more, Joey was smart enough to fake himself an anxiety sickness. Got the Doc to per-scribe him a buncha relaxin' pills. Never took a single one, no sir. Just put 'em in his dates' drinks. Made things go a whole lot easier with the girls, that's fer damn sure!

There's only one unit left in the trailer park fer Joey and Randy to check. The one that's painted faggy blue. Number 1986. Joey hangs back a step as Randy kicks in the door. Jackpot! There's a biggun on the sofa. Ain't too purdy, but so what? She smiles. Is there somethin' wrong with her? Just sittin' there smilin' in that big ol' ratty nightshirt.

"You ready fer some, bitch?" Randy says. He charges on in.

"Hold on!" Joey shouts.

Soon as Randy steps onto the rug in the entryway, he crashes into the trailer's undercarriage. Only a few foot drop, but damn if he ain't screamin' in pain. Joey steps up to see what's the matter and—ho lee shit! There's metal spikes buried down there, and a bunch of 'em is stickin' right through Randy's legs and feet. That fat cow gone and made herself a goddamn booby trap!

"Get me outta here!" Randy says.

"Fuck, man. That smell. You crap yerself?"

"It's these spikes! They're smeared with shit! Get me out!"

Instead of offerin' Randy a hand, Joey aims his assault rifle at his buddy and blows him to kingdom come.

If that seems cruel, you gotta try an' understand. Randy was real close to turnin' full-on zombie. Now with him wounded, he'd be slowin' Joey down on top of it. It was time fer Joey to put the guy outta his misery and get him outta his hair. Now Joey can be a lone wolf, which is just how he likes it.

"That trap was kinda smart," Joey tells the woman. She hasn't moved, still sittin' there and smilin' like a moron. "But it was also kinda dumb. Good fer one intruder, but what if there's more'n one? Like me." He steps 'round the hole in the floor and makes his way towards her, real slow like, watchin' fer more booby traps 'long the way. Just like Randy shoulda done. He was a moron, too.

A puppet show is playin' on the TV. Joey 'members it from back when he was a kid. What were the names of them stupid ragdolls again? They live together an' are always goin' at it like an old married couple. Prob'ly a couple of fags. Joey shuts off the TV and sets his rifle 'gainst it. It ain't like the woman is goin' nowhere—nowhere fast, at least.

"We can do this easy or hard. You can lay back and enjoy, or I can punch yer ugly face. What's it gonna be?"

She hitches up her nightshirt. Looks like she ain't wearin' no panties, but it's hard to tell with her belly fat hangin' down there. She hitches that up, too.

Joey drops his pants to his ankles and waddles up to her. Goddamn he's hard! Never used to get this hard before the Sis. Must be what it's like when you take them little blue boner pills. He bends down and tries to find his way inside her. It helps that she's pullin' up all them flaps of skin, but you still gotta know yer way 'round. There's some hit-and-miss and then he's in. After one thrust, Joey knows somethin' ain't right. It hurts like hell, like he stuck his pecker in a bramble bush.

"Fuck!"

He tries to pull out but he's stuck. Any move he makes brings another jolt of pain. And damn if that bitch don't go right on smilin'.

"What's wrong with yer pussy? Fuck! What's wrong with it?"

Joey gives a real good tug, and he's free of her. He's got some kinda contraption on his dick, kinda like a condom but bigger, thicker, more solid. There's writin' on it: PETER EATER® RAPE TRAP. He yanks at it, and GODDAMN that hurts. It won't come off. Blood starts leakin' down his shaft.

The woman pulls off her nightshirt, and Joey sees that she's covered with tumors—lumps upon lumps upon lumps. Like the blob! She's got the Sis—*real bad*. Lickety-split she's on top of Joey (she can move purdy damn fast, after all). She pins him to the floor, smotherin' him, humpin' him like he's a giant fuck pillow. Joey can't breathe. He bites into them tumor sacks that're all over his face, but it don't stop her from grindin' on him like a bitch in heat, just gives him a mouthful of blood and goop and sweat. Joey is fadin' fast. In a way, he's glad he's goin' out like this. At least it's a woman rapin' him to death, not Randy.

Joey Cologne ain't no homo.

CHAPTER 17

A five-minute walk along the boulevard brings Hank to JG McGator's. The parking lot is an assortment of cars and dump runners—not many customers, thankfully. Hank makes his way inside and is accosted by a hostess wearing a green foam hat shaped like an alligator's head. She's young, early twenties.

"Chompity-chomp, sir! What are you looking to take a bite out of this evening?"

Hank isn't positive, but he thinks he's getting a whiff of shit off of her. "Scotch. I'd like a big bite of Scotch."

"Fantastic! Head on over to the Swamp!" She points to the restaurant's bar area, which is decorated to look like an old bayou shack. A fan boat sticks out of the wall, creating the illusion (somewhat) that it came crashing through the building.

"I need to take a leak first," Hank says.

"The privies are around the corner."

"Privies?"

"Outhouses. Toilets."

"They're not really outhouses, are they?"

"Don't be silly, sir. Have yourself a nice pee. But watch out for gators. Chompity-chomp!"

Christ.

Hank walks down a hallway that ends with two doors. One has a picture of an alligator wearing a top hat, monocle, and moustache. The other shows an alligator with a red bow on its head and long eyelashes. Hank opens the first door expecting to enter the lap of luxury, like at the monorail station. He walks into a disaster area instead. Half of the restroom's fluorescent lights are out, and the remaining ones are flashing on and off at sporadic intervals. The walls are spotted with mold. There are puddles all over the floor that Hank prays are water. He splashes through them on his way to the urinals for what he's hoping will be the world's fastest whizz. He passes a man standing at one of the sinks, dressed in a suit and wearing a crown. Birthday party, maybe? The guy is coughing and hacking like he has bronchitis.

Lovely.

The back wall of each of the four urinals is streaked with rust. They look like they should be condemned, but Hank isn't about to check and see what the toilets in the stalls look like. He chooses the right-most urinal at random and gets to it. As he does, the man at the sink keeps coughing. It sounds like he's trying (and failing) to hock up something from deep in his throat. He's practically choking! Hank is worried he'll have to stop his piss mid-stream and give the guy the Heimlich.

As Hank finishes and zips up, it sounds like the guy has finally gotten the best of his loogie. He spits and spits and spits in victory.

Absolutely lovely.

Hank goes to the sinks to wash his hands and gets his first good look at Mr. Hacker: Fifties. Red hair. And his mouth ...

What the ...?

His mouth is mottled brown.

Hank stares into the man's sink: It looks like it's been hit with a diarrhea blast. In the middle of the splatter is a big stinking turd. Hank's fight or flight instincts kick in like they did in the sculpture garden, and he knows he needs to retreat—out of the restroom, out of JG McGator's, out of the World Village entirely this time. The Sarge and Stevie can go fuck themselves. He wasn't cut out for this.

Hank heads for the door.

"Mr. Shatley!"

Hank turns and sees that the man is smiling at him. "Who are you? How do you know my name?"

The man's eyes glow red to match his hair. "We need to talk, Mr. Shatley."

From the World Village Rules & Regulations – Harmony Community Association Guidelines:

41.09 – IDOL WORSHIP

As we say in our world of Harmony, you shall keep no graven images, except for those of Al Peora. Here are the instructions for creating and worshipping your Peora idol. Please refer to the HCA's Article 12, Section B, for more information on this subject.

41.09.01 – Toilet Bowl Colanders

All residential toilets in Harmony must be manufactured with, or retrofitted to include, a detachable colander for the bowl. This allows your urine to flow through the perforations while trapping your solid fecal matter.

41.09.02 – Plaster Peora Molds – Delivery and Collection

Every Tuesday, except on designated holidays, plaster Peora molds will be delivered to and collected from residences in

Harmony, as needed. The molds are quarter-scale versions of the magnificent Peora statue that greets travelers at the World Village airport.

41.09.03 – Plaster Peora Molds – Placement

Your plaster Peora mold comes with two stakes, one for each of Peora's feet, to secure the idol to your lawn. The idol should be staked in your front or back yard, in the centermost spot as permitted by your existing landscaping.

41.09.04 – The Creative Process

After a bowel movement, remove your toilet bowl colander and take your excrement to your Peora idol. Smear the excrement over the plaster. Your goal, over time, is to cover the idol completely. How long this takes will depend on the number of people at your residence, your diet(s), and your frequency of defecation. Remember: This isn't a race! The idol will be covered when it's covered. In the meantime, have fun and be creative. Include as many bells and whistles as you can think of. Maybe you could use your fingernail to detail each pinstripe on Peora's suit. If you should happen to have a bloody stool one day, that would be an excellent opportunity to add some color to your sculpture and give Peora that beautiful shock of red hair He's known for. Make your neighbors jealous—the sky's the limit!

41.09.05 – Worship

After each application of excrement, please take a few minutes to worship your Peora idol. Thank Him for His kindness. For His generosity. For His compassion. Thank Him for creating the World Village. Thank Him for surrounding it with a great and beautiful wall. Thank Him for protecting you from the horrors of the outside world. Protecting you from ANSIS. Protecting you from Asians. Protecting you from turd-fearing radicals. Praise Him! Praise each of His creations. Praise DoodyWorld. Praise DingleBush Gardens. Praise Him and Praise

Him again, for He gives you so much! He gives you the curiosity to discover what's popular in His world. He gives you the tenacity to follow the trends. He gives you all of this and more. He even gives you nü metal!!! He invented it. Anyone who says nü metal existed before He was born is lying. Ask Carl Tuchus—he'll give you the straight poop. Poop be praised! Peora be praised! Hallelujah and Amen.

41.09.06 – Completion

All Harmony residents will receive a gold crown (a replica of the one Al Peora wears when He's out and about). When your Peora idol is entirely covered in excrement and customized to your satisfaction, place the crown on His head. This will signal that it's time for your idol to be collected and a new plaster mold delivered. For more details, refer to Section 41.09.02 – Plaster Peora Molds – Delivery and Collection.

Dear John,

This is the hardest letter I've ever had to write. I don't mean to hurt you, but I don't think we should see each other anymore. I'm sorry. Maybe I should have listened to Doris. She thought we were wrong for each other from the start. She said a woman like me had no business getting involved with a Porta John like you. But our time together has truly been wonderful, my dearest John.

I know that ours hasn't been an exclusive relationship. I've never expected you to be loyal to me and me alone when you're stationed at that construction site, not with so many bare, beautiful bottoms being planted on you every day. To be honest, it excites me to think about you getting filled up by all those men. When I visit you at night, after the workers are gone, I can't contain myself. I love giving you a rimjob, licking you clean of every stray drop of pee, and then sticking my hand deep inside you and noodling around in the muck. It's pure heaven. So you're probably wondering, why not continue as we have been? Well, I've started seeing someone else, and when I tell you who it is, I think you'll understand.

It's Al Peora.

I know. I can hardly believe it myself. When I moved to the World Village, my son, rest his soul, accused me of having a crush on Al. I denied it, but I *did* have a crush on him, of course! What woman doesn't? I would never have imagined he'd be interested in a biddy like me. But we've gone out several times now, and he makes me feel special. He treats me like I'm a piece of shit. We go for drives in his dump runner, and he takes me to dinner at KFC. He has lots of cute pet names for me, too, like horseface and stupid cow.

I love him.

Please don't hate me, John. I pray you'll understand. You're full of shit, but Al is the shittiest. He's shit personified. I want to be with him, exclusively.

I wish you nothing but happiness and hope this letter finds you well. Actually, I hope it finds you, period. I called the number on your door (1-800-POOPIES), and they gave me the mailing address for Discount Portable Toilets LLC. I trust someone will read my note to you. If not, then you probably *will* hate me, never knowing why I abandoned you. Either way, our late-night rendepoos are over.

I hope you can forgive me, my sweet, sweet John. Maybe we can remain friends? If not, I understand.

Take care of yourself,

Emma

CARL TUCHUS, CHANNEL 2 NEWS:

Good evening and welcome to *Talking Shit*. I'm your host, Carl Tuchus.

I hope that all of you had a great weekend. As for myself, I participated in runDoody, the annual DoodyWorld marathon event. I finished in a little over four hours, which isn't too shabby. Granted, I ran in the 5K race, not the full marathon, but that's still an impressive time for a bloated old dog like me. I was drenched in sweat when I crossed the finish line, and I was expecting to be greeted with a round of applause. But instead, I was arrested, taken to jail, and fined five hundred dollars for public perspiration.

Okay, maybe I'm fibbing a little. Let's back up.

I *did* run in the DoodyWorld 5K. And I *was* sweating profusely. But I wasn't arrested, jailed, or fined. My question is: Why not? If America's poop police applied their same standards to all types of bodily discharges, I most certainly would have been. But the poop police don't care about your sweat. They don't care about your blood or tears, either. All they care about is your poop. Everything else that comes from your body is wonderful. A miracle. But not your poop. Your poop is evil, they say. It stinks. It's dirty. It can even ... KILL YOU!

All of that is complete hogwash. Obviously. You know it. I know it. Even the lying poop police know it. How did we get to the point where millions of Americans accept these bald-faced lies as gospel truth? Because we've been conditioned to accept them, quite literally, from birth. Most babies are fitted with their first diaper within minutes of emerging from the womb. The new parents sit there and watch the nurse do it, smiles on their faces. Would they sit and smile if the nurse put a bag over their newborn's head? No, I suspect they would rip her a new one for doing something so humiliating. And that's precisely how they should react when their baby is being diapered, because it's every bit as disgraceful. Instead, they start poop-shaming their baby themselves, keeping their child in senseless and demeaning diapers for years.

But it doesn't stop there. Oh no, not by a longshot. When the parents can no longer demean their children, they start demeaning themselves. The U.S. adult diaper industry surpassed twenty-five million dollars last year. Think about it: Grown men and women are walking around with a load in their pants, not saying a word, acting as if their poop is a shameful secret instead of something to be proud of.

Hold on, you say. Adult diapers aren't only for poop. They're for urinary incontinence, too. Technically that's true, but the poop police don't look at poop and pee the same way. Nowhere is this more evident than in the world of adult entertainment. Go to your favorite porn site, and you'll find tens of thousands of watersports videos. A search for scat videos, on the other hand, will yield zero results. The implication is clear: Watching people take a piss is sexy; watching people take a poop is obscene. When all is said and done, you can pee all over the place and the poop police don't care. Pee in the street. Pee in the stairwell. Pee in the snow. People do it all the time. But don't you dare poop! Well, I have a message for the poop police: You're fighting a losing battle. You'll never regulate people's natural bodily functions, and you have no right to. God didn't put diapers on Adam and Eve, did he? You know why? Because it's our God-given right to take a shit, whenever and wherever we choose to. Just like it's my God-given right to talk about shit. I do it for sixty minutes, every weeknight, right on this very program. And I'll continue to do so until the poop police finally release their stranglehold on America's bowels. That's my solemn promise to each and every one of you, my loyal viewers.

I'm Carl Tuchus, and *Talking Shit* will return— Khoff! Ahem. Excuse me.

Khoff! Khoff! Ahem. Kaff! Khak! Ptui! Khoff! Khoff! Ach-tooey! Ach-tooey! Ahem.

(TUCHUS POINTS TO THE TURD ON HIS DESK)

I suppose I should be ashamed of that, too. Huh, poop police? Maybe we should all start wearing mouth diapers. You people are pathetic.

Talking Shit will return right after these messages from our sponsors.

ON-SCREEN GRAPHIC:

COMING UP | THE CHANGE: CRAZY RUMOR OR ALREADY HAPPENING?

CHAPTER 18

2018:

The thing that struck Hank the most about Neon City was the streets. All of them were wet, soaked with huge puddles of water. Looking down at the city from the limousine, Hank was mesmerized by the brilliant neon reflections shimmering on the asphalt.

"How do the streets get so wet with no rain?" Hanks asked.

"The roadways have an underground irrigation system," Liz said.

"What for?"

"No purpose. Peora just likes the look of wet streets." Liz sat in the limo seat across from Hank, not bothering to take in the view. All business, this one.

Hank and Liz were on their way to Manufacture, a punk rock club on Ocean Boulevard. Hank felt silly wearing his old wardrobe: white linen suit, pastel blue t-shirt, and white braided loafers (without socks, naturally). But this was what Peora insisted he wear, so that was that. Liz was going to fit in better with her purple mohawk, hot pink jumpsuit, and black ankle boots. She looked like a new wave astronaut and a damn sexy one at that. *Behave,* Hank reminded himself. He was pretty sure that Liz could kill him a hundred different ways using nothing but one of her oversized earrings. No need to find out.

The limo started to descend from its flying lane. Manufacture had to be one of the neon-lit, art deco-style buildings below.

"We'll be landing in a minute," the driver announced.

This was all so surreal! Hank had to keep reminding himself that he was in Iowa—an enormous stretch of cornfields that Peora terraformed into a *Miami Vice*-inspired retro paradise. There was even an artificial ocean with mechanically generated tides. An impenetrable dome covered everything in Neon City, protecting Peora from the beings he'd ripped off and double-crossed in other galaxies.

"Are you ready?" Liz asked.

"I don't know."

"Play it cool. Peora thinks you're the greatest. He loves *Frankenstein 1986*. Let him fawn all over you while I do my thing."

"Which is ...?"

"Just get me to Peora," she said.

As the limo touched ground, Hank noticed that the marquee in front of the venue was stacked with band names. He remembered some of them from back in the 80s. The band members would have to be in their sixties by now. Hank wondered if the actual bands were playing or if it would be a bunch of Peora's biomechs on stage. He'd find out soon enough.

The limo doors opened, and Hank and Liz were greeted by three Grays wearing black militaristic uniforms. They had bulbous bald heads and large black eyes.

"Hank Bell?" one of them asked.

"Yes."

"I am Beopa." The alien looked at Liz but continued speaking to Hank. "Who is the female?"

"That's my assistant, Liz. She travels everywhere with me. I can't match my socks without her." Hank wiggled a sockless ankle outside the car door. "Little joke."

The Grays conferred for a moment, and then Beopa said, "Come with us."

Hank and Liz followed the Grays through the crowd gathered outside the club. Everyone appeared to be in compliance with Neon City's dress code: 1) 80s-appropriate attire only, and 2) NO EARTH TONES. It was impossible know if the clubgoers were Peora's guests or biomechs. Probably a mix. Whatever they were, Liz got some whistles and catcalls. All Hank got was a snide comment from one joker: "Well, if it isn't Don Johnson."

Inside the club, the bass-thumping wall behind the crowded bar told Hank that a band was playing in the next room.

"Wait here," Beopa said. "I will let Peora know you have arrived."

A television above the bar showed a Lakers-Celtics game. Hank watched as Larry Bird hit a jump shot. "Everything is retro, huh?"

"The game is live," Liz said. "Right down the street at the Pro Sports Arena. Peora has engineered all of his favorite teams."

"Wow."

"The big question is whether we're really meeting with Peora or if it'll be one of his doubles. He's looking forward to meeting you, so I'm hoping it's him."

"So you can kill him?"

"Stop. I'm not even armed."

"Yeah, but those earrings."

"What?"

"Never mind."

Beopa returned. "He will see you now. But first ..." The alien held a wand device in front of Hank and Liz and ran it from head to toe over both of them. "Okay. Follow me."

"Told you I'm clean," Liz whispered to Hank.

Beopa took them to where the band was playing. The stage was decorated with barbed wire and sandbags. Between the strobe lights and the fog machine, it was hard to see the band members. From the glimpses Hank got through the glowing, pulsing vapor, they looked twentyish. Biomechs, for sure. They sounded great, though. Hank recognized the song they were playing, and it was a spot-on rendition.

Hank and Liz followed Beopa along the periphery of the rowdy, moshing crowd until they reached the other side of the room. They walked up two flights of stairs and exited into a pink-painted hallway. Beopa led Hank and Liz to the door at the end of the hall and opened it for them. They stepped into a huge vaulted office decorated with glass blocks and neon galore. All of the furniture was brightly colored and minimalist in design, including the desk where Peora sat. His general appearance was similar to the other aliens, except he had tufts of red hair on top of his head and he wore a Hawaiian shirt.

"Mr. Bell!" Peora said. He stood to greet his guests, revealing that he was also wearing white dress slacks. "It is an honor to finally meet you."

"The honor is mine," Hank said.

"I had the hardest time tracking you down."

"Sorry. I haven't used my stage name in forever. These days I'm Hank Shatley, realtor extraordinaire."

"You no longer act? But why?"

"*Frankenstein 1986* kind of killed my career."

"I do not understand. You were brilliant."

"Well, thank you. People didn't like the idea of Frankenstein in Versace, I guess."

"It is one of my top five movies of all time."

"Wow. What are the other four?"

"The *Miami Vice* pilot, *Scarface*, *Band of the Hand*, and *Cobra*. When I intercepted the broadcasts of those movies, it inspired me to travel to your planet. But when I arrived last year, I found something so very different from what I had seen. So I re-created the world I fell in love with, here in Neon City."

"It's amazing. Beautiful!"

"Speaking of beautiful, who is your companion?"

"This is my assistant, Liz Herro. I hope you don't mind that she joined me. I always travel with her."

Peora took Liz's offered hand and kissed it with his lipless mouth. "How could I mind the company of someone so lovely?"

"Thank you," Liz said.

To Hank's surprise, that's all she said. He couldn't figure out what she was up to. If she wasn't here to kill Peora or deliver a message to him, then what was the point of all this?

"Could you do me a favor?" Peora asked Hank.

"Sure."

"It would fill me with happiness if you would serenade me with 'Pulse of Miami.'"

Ugh. Of all of Hank's embarrassing memories associated with *Frankenstein 1986*, that song was the worst of them. The producers were looking for a tie-in single to promote the film, so they worked in a scene where Frankenstein sings a synthpop song in a Miami nightclub. Instead of a hit, they got a horrible song, in a horrible movie, sung horribly flat. (Hank told the producers again and again that he didn't have a voice, but they wouldn't listen to him.)

"I ... don't really remember the words," Hank said.

"I can get them for you."

"Well ..."

"Maybe just a verse or two?"

"I don't know ..."

"It would not have to be right now. But sometime this evening?"

"Let me think about it."

"Yes! You think about it. Wonderful. For now, I have something to show you. Come with me into the next room."

"Is there a bathroom around here?" Liz asked.

"Yes, back out in the hallway. Beopa will take you there."

While Beopa escorted Liz through the doorway they came from, Peora led Hank to another door across the room. "After you."

Hank walked into an entertainment room equipped with a full bar, pool table, and jukebox. The amenities were overshadowed by a massive pile of white power—presumably cocaine—in the middle of the room. It reached from the floor to the ceiling!

"Welcome to Snow White Mountain!" Peora said.

"Christ."

"Would you care to go on an expedition?"

"Sorry, I have to pass. I did some coke in the 80s. But not anymore. I'd be up for weeks."

"You could always count sheep. Baaaaaah! Or mountain goats. Right?"

Hank thought that Peora was making a joke, but he wasn't positive. He didn't want to laugh and insult him, so he said, "That's right."

"How about we hit the town together in my Daytona Spyder? Maybe stop in at the Arc Light? It is an exact replica of the arcade featured in Season 2, Episode 21 of *Miami Vice*. Do you like to play Tempest?"

"Yeah, sure."

"Excellent! But there is one thing I need you to do for me first."

"Like I said, I'll think about the song."

"No, no. Not that. I need you to tell me about your female companion. Who is she?"

Hank felt his heart drop into his stomach. "What do you mean?"

"She is not your assistant. Who is she with? The CIA? NSA?"

Hank said nothing.

"I am not mad at you, Mr. Bell. I have no doubt that you are a pawn in this game, that she approached you about our visit. I do not blame you for going along with whatever she proposed. It is difficult to say no to a powerful government agent. I understand. But I do need you to tell me the truth. Please—do not force me to go down the path of *making* you tell me. It would ruin the special evening I have planned for us."

"I ..." Hank didn't know what to do.

"NOBODY MOVE!"

Liz stood in the doorway, holding a scary-ass knife—black and shiny and jagged—like something a ninja assassin would use.

Peora seemed puzzled, and then a smile spread across his face. "Fecal rites, Ms. Herro? You are a clever one, my dear, whoever you are."

"What's going on?" Hank asked.

"It appears as though your lovely companion was making poops and casting spells in the bathroom."

Liz flung the knife at Peora. Before Hank could blink, it was buried up to the handle in the alien's right arm.

"SHAZBOT!" Peora yelled, grimacing in pain. He groped behind his back with an unsteady hand. "Too bad about your aim."

"No worries." Liz produced two more knives from an oversized pocket on her jumpsuit. "I made lots of poops." She fired the knives in rapid succession before Peora could get to his weapon. This time they both hit their mark—one in Peora's stomach, the other in his chest.

Peora stared at his wounds and then at Hank. "I ... I hear music ... Our theme song, I think ..."

"I don't understand," Hank said.

The alien collapsed, green blood spilling onto the floor. He was the real deal, not a biomech.

Liz smiled at Hank. "We did it!"

"*We?* Did *what?*"

"Isn't it obvious?"

"You said you weren't going to kill him!"

Suddenly, Liz looked worried—afraid, even. "Wait ... Is this right?" She sounded like a nervous teenager, totally unsure of herself.

"Is *what* right?"

She took a couple of steps back, her eyes shifting from Hank, to Peora's body on the floor, to the mountain of cocaine. "Is any of this even right?"

"What do you mean?"

"Where's Emma?"

"Huh?"

Shouting now: "WHERE'S EMMA?"

She's losing it, Hank thought.

Liz sat cross-legged on the floor. She wrapped her arms around her knees, rocked back and forth, and started muttering to herself. "Who am I? Where am I? What am I doing here? Who am I? Where am I? What am I doing here?"

Correction: She's lost it.

She closed her eyes, and an orange glow began to radiate around her.

"Who am I? Where am I? What am I doing here?"

The orange glow intensified.

"Who am I? Where am I? What am I doing here?"

Expanded.

"Who am I? Where am I? What am I doing here?"

Enveloped Liz in a sun-like sphere.

"Who am I? Where am I? What am I doing here?"

In a flashbang instant, the orb was gone.

And so was Liz.

Just you and me again, Shitley.

That voice in Hank's head. He had heard it before. He was sure of it. But who was it?

Three Grays charged into the room, blast guns in hand. Nothing to see here, boys. Just your dead leader with a bunch of knives sticking out of him. A dead guard in the hall with his neck slit open. And visiting dignitary Hank Bell, star of *Frankenstein 1986*, left to take the fall.

"Put your hands up, Mr. Bell! Do not make any sudden movements, or we will fire."

Even though Hank was royally fucked, he couldn't help but recite his line, in character, from *Frankenstein 1986:* "Fire ... bad."

CHAPTER 19

America after the Change is a return to discipline: Redneck baby daddy crams a loaded diaper into his toddler's mouth to toilet train him. A return to religion: Shit God, Piss Christ. A return to morals: Do you have a face like a twelve-pound boiled ham? Sign up today for the Carl Tuchus lookalike contest! The Change is mountains of dog mess. Dead animals rotting in manure fields. Turds in the punchbowl. Scarab-faced good ol' boys head on down to the local swimmin' hole. They dig in the mud for fossilized feces until the dinner bell calls 'em home. Running barefoot past broken trampolines and a burning fertilizer plant. A pompadoured charlatan and his horse-toothed blonde assistant sell a wonder tonic from the back of their huckster wagon. "This here potion will cure bronchitis, hepatitis, encephalitis, and even near-sightedness!" It's nothing but bottled farts, but people line up for it at every stop, waving American flags and handfuls of money. Ah, the country life. Just one o' them days, I guess. Beats living in the cities, though. They're nothing but poop-filled prisons—same basic design as 1940s Japanese internment camps, but on a larger scale. SHART protestors are washed away by a tsunami of sewage. There's been an exponential rise in poo-related crimes since the Change.

Everything from serial poopers to one-off incidents. POLICE: Macy's employee splashes co-worker with jar full of feces & urine. Ain't life grand? Ain't capitalism grand? Gotta rig the system to keep it running. Shit-stuff the ballot boxes. Shit-smear the opposition. Do whatever it takes to win, up to and including wastewaterboarding. God Bless America! Pack up the kids and fly to DoodyWorld. First stop: the Hall of Assholes. It's really something to see all those animatronics on stage; butt cheeks spread to show you their anal warts, anal hemorrhoids, anal herpes, anal cancer, anal bleeding, and anal fissures. So many fucking assholes! That's what the Change is all about. The Change is football goalposts covered with crap. *(The kick is up, and it's ... no good! Just a shit wide to the right.)* Dump runner drag races. Shitcoin blackmail schemes. If you think that poo's rad, then swim in the Duad. That's what we used to say when I was in grade school. Vagabond rat boys leaping into the river like lemmings. We're all watching for secret signals, listening for tribal drumming in the night. I wander the streets for hours, looking at rust stains on the crumbling buildings. There's this one—if I stare at it long enough, I swear I can see the faces of fourteen babies, eyes sewn shut, sticking out their long lizard tongues at me. The door has an engraved circle with a square inside, along with some other weird markings. I want to knock *(don't do it ... just walk away)*, but I can't bring myself to.

I can't get that building off my mind. The one with the strange door. A square inside a circle. It seems like it means something.

My best guess is that the building is a weigh station for uterine tumors. Those things are HOT right now; the heavier the fibroid, the higher the price. An investment banker in Helsinki, Finland, recently paid over two million dollars for a 120-pound tumor that encompassed a woman's entire abdominal cavity. With that kind of money at stake, the weights need to be exact. I bet the building is filled with the most expensive scales in the world, along with other types of experimental calibration devices.

That has to be it.

I return to the wastelands, return to the building, but I'm not alone this time. A beautiful woman with wings like a dragon is staring at the door, examining the symbols. She's wearing a black latex bodysuit. Come to think of it, so am I.

"Has this place been calling to you?" she asks me.

"Yeah. What do you think it is?"

"If I had to guess, I'd say it has something to do with uterine tumors."

"That's exactly what I thought! Maybe we should just ... knock?"

"No."

"Why not?"

"I was told not to. By the voice in my head. Your brain is talking to you, too, isn't it?"

(nothing to see here ... move along ... please return home ... all is well)

"Yes ... What's going on? Do you want to get a cup of guano with me? Maybe if we think this through together, we can figure things out."

"Sorry, not interested. If I had met you a week ago, possibly. But not now. Sometimes timing is everything."

"But—"

She spreads her wings and flies away.

CHAPTER 20

HANK & AL

Starring in ...

"BARNYARD BEDDY-BYE"

Hank and Al are in their twin beds, a nightstand and lamp separating the two. Hank's bed has an H on the headboard, and Al's has an A. Al is lying on his side with his eyes closed; Hank is on his back, eyes wide open.

HANK: Al? Hey, Al! Are you awake?

AL:(opening his eyes) Now I am. What do you want, Hank?

HANK: I can't sleep, Al.

Al sits up in bed. His sleep-worn red hair sticks out in all directions.

AL: Count sheep then, Hank.

HANK: Count sheep?

AL: Yes, Hank.

HANK: Okay, Al. I'll give it a try.

Al lies down and closes his eyes.

A sheep prances into the room.

SHEEP: BAAAAAAAH!!!

Al jerks upright. The sheep hurdles over the beds and exits the room.

HANK: One!

Another sheep enters, bleats loudly, jumps the beds, and leaves.

HANK: Two!

Another sheep does the same.

HANK: Three!

AL: (yelling) Hank, stop it!

HANK: What's wrong, Al? You told me to count sheep.

AL:I know I did, Hank. Have a glass of warm milk instead. That'll help you fall asleep.

HANK: Warm milk?

AL: Yes, Hank.

HANK: Okay, Al. Whatever you say.

Hank gets out of bed and leaves the room. Al lies down and closes his eyes. Hank returns, holding a bucket and leading a cow on a rope. He kneels next to the cow, puts the bucket under its udder, and starts milking.

COW: MOOOOOOO!!!

Al opens his eyes. Hank keeps milking.

COW: MOOOOOOO!!!

Al sits up. Hank keeps milking.

COW: MOOOOOOO!!!

AL: (yelling) Hank!

HANK: What's wrong, Al?

AL: What in the world are you doing?

HANK: I'm getting some milk from this cow, so I can warm it up and have a glass. Just like you told me to.

AL: That's going to take forever! Try listening to music. Something nice and pleasant.

HANK: Will do, Al.

Hank takes the cow out of the room and gets back into bed. Al lies down and closes his eyes.

Three mice and a brightly colored bird enter the room. The mice carry guitar, bass, and drums, and the bird holds a microphone.

They launch into a punk rendition of "Down by the Old Mill Stream."

BIRD: Down by the old mill stream!

That's where I heard you scream!

I smashed your face to goo!

And then I ate it too!

For it was there I knew!

That you did love me true!

AL: (yelling) Stop it! Stop it! Stop it!

HANK: What's wrong, Al?

AL: That song is terrible! I told you to listen to something nice and pleasant.

HANK: OH! I thought you said something with *mice and pheasant*.

AL: No, no, no!

HANK: Sorry about that, Al. But you know what? That music did make me kind of tired. I think I'm ready to go to sleep now.

AL: Finally!

The animals leave the room. Hank lies down and closes his eyes.

HANK: Good night, Al.

Al lies down and closes his eyes.

AL: Good night, Hank.

Al opens his eyes.

AL: Fooey! I have to go to the bathroom.

Al is about to step out of bed, but he stops before his foot hits the floor. The carpet is covered with poop from all the animals.

AL: Hank! There's doody everywhere!

Hank doesn't stir.

AL: Hank! You have to clean this up!

Hank starts to snore—-he's in a DEEP sleep.

AL: HANK!

The snoring gets louder.

AL: HAAAAAAAAAAAAAAAANK!!!
A trombone makes a long, sad wah-wah-wah sound.
"Hank and Al's Theme" plays for the outro.

CHAPTER 21

1985:

Harold was shooting pool in the rec center when Hank walked in holding a packet of papers. His forlorn expression didn't look promising.

"So ...?" Harold asked. "What's the verdict?"

"General discharge," Hank said.

"What? Not honorable?"

"They call it a general discharge under honorable conditions."

"That's bullshit."

"I'll take it. I'm just glad there won't be an inquest."

"What are you going to do? Head out to Hollywood? You've sure talked about it enough."

"I don't know. I know what the Sarge will be doing. Spending the rest of his life in a chair."

"You can't be so hard on yourself. Have you talked with him?"

"He says he doesn't blame me. Made me promise to get help with my poo issue."

"There you go. Get that taken care of, and then you can have a fresh start. I'll be seeing you on the big screen in no time."

"I'm gonna go pack up."

"How about a final game of foosball first?"

Hank smiled. It was the first genuine smile Harold had seen on him in weeks.

"Okay, Hairy Man," Hank said. "I suppose I can kick your hairy ass one last time."

1986:

Stevie was starting to drift off to sleep when he realized someone else was in the refrigerator with him. Someone with long hair and soft skin.

"Mom ...?"

"No. I'm not your mom."

"Who are you?"

"I don't know. Where are we?"

"In my Aunt Cathy's refrigerator. I came in here to hide. Just for fun. But now I can't get out."

"I'm hiding too. Not for fun. Someone's chasing me. All over the world."

"Who?"

"I don't know. A monster, I think. He gets inside me sometimes."

"That sounds scary."

"It is."

"I'm waiting for my dad to get me out of here. Then he can protect you. He's in the Army."

"Thanks. You're sweet. I might have a way to get out. But not through the door. Through time. It's hard to explain, and I'm not sure if I can do it. But if I can, I'll take you with me."

"Okay."

A minute later, the inside of the refrigerator lit up with an orange glow.

Stevie wasn't awake to see it.

CI: Let's go back to what you touched on a few minutes ago. Your first day of junior high school.

HS: I took a shit that morning, and I couldn't get myself clean. I kept wiping and wiping and wiping—so much that the toilet paper started to have spots of blood on it. But there was still brown on it, too. I couldn't figure out what was going on, and I was freaking out. God, I was so stupid. I had goddamned dingleberries. Except I didn't know what those were. I had never been hairy enough before to have one. But now that I was getting hairier, everywhere, some of my shit was smeared into my ass hair. I needed to get my butt back into the shower.

CI: Did you?

HS: Eventually. I was gonna be late for school. I needed to catch my bus. I thought maybe things would just ... fix themselves. Yeah, no. I got laughed at all day. Everyone told me I stank like shit, started calling me Shitley. When I got home, my underwear was filthy. That's when I knew I had to do something. I showered for an hour, but even that didn't take care of it. I had to get in there with scissors and cut the crap out.

CI: How did that go?

HS: Bad. Really, really bad.

CI: Okay, we'll stop there for a short coffee break. When we resume, we'll dig deeper into that incident and how it affected you. We'll also continue to explore your middle school years.

HS: What happens when we reach the end?

CI: The end?

HS: The end of my memories.

CI: We start from the beginning.

HS: Over and over?

CI: Yes.

HS: This isn't my first deposition, is it?

CI: No.

HS: How many times have I done this?

CI: The number is beyond counting. Like the sand of the sea.

HS: And there's nothing more to this?

CI: What do you mean? Like what?

HS: I don't know. Flames? Erupting volcanoes? Rivers of lava?

CI: For some people, sure. Not for you. This is your own personal Hell.

HS: You're saying this is the worst thing for me? Worse than burning alive?

CI: Yes.

HS: That's crazy.

CI: Is it? You'll have to work on sounding more convincing.

CHAPTER 22

Liz is halfway up the walk to Doris's front door when it hits her. A tremendous sense of déjà vu. The feeling is absurd because she knows she's never been here before. She hasn't been *anywhere* before except inside Ryan's head and her DUNG Center prison cell (plus a brief appearance at the Chocolate Starfish concert, but she was so out of it that she barely remembers that). She's still barefoot and wearing her orange jumpsuit. She tried willing herself a new outfit when she projected herself here, but it didn't work. At least she didn't arrive in her birthday suit, like at the concert. It's going to be hard enough for Liz to explain to Ryan's mom how her dead daughter is alive again without being naked on top of it.

Liz rings the front bell on the ranch-style house, and a white-haired woman opens the door. She's dressed all in black: corset, panties, stockings, and heels.

Holy prunetang! Is this Doris?

"Umm, hi ... Are you Ms. Akin?" Liz asks.

"Yes ..."

"Is Emma here?"

"Is it something important? We're in the middle of entertaining." Loud noises come from the back of the house—talking, laughter, music.

"It's, like, really super important."

"Well, okay. Come on in, hun. I'll take you to her."

Liz follows Doris through a house decorated with an abundance of floral patterns and stuffed full of knick-knacks. The little-old-lady sensibilities end when they reach the enclosed lanai, and Liz suddenly feels like she's in a porno flick. There are dozens of people in the sunroom, men and women, and they're all wearing fetish clothing or lingerie, except for the ones who aren't wearing anything. They're lounging on patio furniture and frolicking in the pool. Making out in the hot tub and pushing each other on play swings. Chimpanzees wearing wigs and cocktail dresses walk among the partygoers with serving trays, offering them champagne and hors d'oeuvres. This all seems so over the top, Liz thinks. Is this right? Is this how it was the last time?

Wait ... The last time ...?

That weird déjà vu again. I haven't been here before, Liz reminds herself. *Jeez!*

A robot dressed in a tuxedo approaches Liz. "Hello, ma'am. I'm ANDRE, your Auto-Narrated Decadent Reverie Experience. The games are about to begin. May I fetch you a laxative? Or perhaps some S&M gear?"

"Get bent, C-3PO."

"She's not a guest, ANDRE," Doris says. "Go find Emma for us, will you?"

"Yes, ma'am."

"Why would I want a laxative?" Liz asks.

"We're getting ready to play Shit on a Shingle."

"What's that?"

"Oh, it's the most wonderful party game. You put a piece of toast in the middle of the room, and everyone takes a fast-acting laxative. The goal is to see long how you can hold your bowels. When you can't do it anymore, you relieve yourself on the toast. The person who lasts the longest gets to eat the toast with all the toppings."

"*Gets to?* That's a reward?"

"Don't tell me you've never partaken in poop! Maybe you'd like to join us."

"Gross-o-rama."

Doris laughs. "To each their own! I can't bring myself to eat a snail, and yet I know plenty of people who adore escargot. Go figure, right?"

ANDRE returns with another white-haired woman. This has to be Emma! She looks exactly like Liz would expect, based on her shared memories from Ryan, except for the fact that she's wearing crotchless fishnet pantyhose and a cupless harness bra.

"Liz! It's so good to see you. Give me a hug, dear."

O-kay. Liz thought that Emma might scream when she saw her. Or pass out. Or both. "You don't seem surprised I'm here."

"Why should I be?"

"Because I'm dead?"

"Miracles happen all the time in the World Village. I knew you'd show up one day." Emma turns to Doris. "This is my daughter, Liz."

"Your daughter who died all those years ago?" Doris takes Liz's hand. "I had no idea it was you, hun. So great to meet you!"

This doesn't make sense. Why is everyone being so nonchalant? Liz decides to go along with it. She's not going to get into the whole I'm-kind-of-your-daughter-but-not-really thing with Emma. Better to let her think she's her daughter than a thoughtform made flesh. She might have a better chance of convincing her to leave the World Village this way.

"Nice to meet you, too," Liz tells Doris. And then to Emma: "Can we talk in private for a minute?"

"Yes. But where's my hug first?"

Liz hesitates for a second and then wilts into Emma's arms. She feels like she could cry. After spending a month in a tiny prison cell, Liz didn't realize how badly she needed a warm embrace. But what about Emma? Why is Liz the only one who's getting weepy here?

"Okay, let's find someplace to talk," Emma says. She leads them out of the lanai, down a hallway, and into a small reading room. "Here we go. One thing: Let's not dredge up the past. All that matters is the here and now. We need to live in the present, launch ourselves on every wave, and find our eternity in each moment."

"That's fine. I need you to do something for me."

"I'd do anything for you, dear."

"Good. I want you to go to the airport with me. I want us to get out of here."

"Here?"

"The World Village."

"Why would we do that?"

Liz needs to be careful. If she tells Emma the truth—that the World Village is controlled by a demon from Hell—she's going to sound like a lunatic. But she has to tell her something. Can she get away with being vague? "I think it's dangerous here. I think something bad is going to happen."

"Oh, no, dear. This is the safest place in the world. We have a glorious wall for protection. Nothing bad is getting in here."

"Something bad is already here!"

"What do you mean?"

"Look around. Look at this party. Shit eating? S&M?"

"We're only having fun."

"But this isn't you!"

"You've been gone a long time. We should get reacquainted before you start telling me what's *me*. Don't you think so?"

"You're right. I *have* been gone a long time. And now I'm back. From the dead. Wearing a prison uniform. Like, *hello?* This doesn't seem mondo bizarro to you?"

"No. Not really."

"Then you're not yourself."

"You sound like your brother."

"I was with Ryan. Right before he died. I came here because he was so worried about you."

"Well, that's sweet that he was worried, but everything is fine."

"Everything is *not* fine! Look, you said you'd do anything for me. I want us to leave here. Are you going back on your word?"

"I'd do anything *reasonable* for you. I had no way of knowing you'd ask me for something so outrageous. I can't just pack up and leave. I'm in a relationship, for heaven's sake."

"A relationship? With who?"

"Al Peora."

"Peora?"

"He's the president of the World Village."

"Yeah, I know who he is. You're dating Al Peora?"

"That sounds like we're in high school. Our love is ... I don't even know how to describe it. It's sweeter than life itself."

"You met the guy once. At JG McGator's. You don't even know him."

"Elizabeth! You're talking to me like I'm senile. Of course I know him. Would you like to meet him?"

"What?"

"He's here."

"At your party?"

"Yes."

Liz can't figure out if Emma could possibly be serious. Al Peora, aka Baal-Peor, aka Belphegor, one of the seven princes of Hell, is loading up a plate full of cocktail weenies in the next room? No fucking way! Then again, with a game like Shit on a Shingle on the agenda, maybe it's not so crazy that the Belphmeister would make an appearance. There's only one way to find out. "Take me to him," she tells Emma.

Back to the lanai they go. Everyone is gathered around a heavyset man, cheering him on as he drops his leather pants and crouches over a piece of toast on the floor. There's a boy in the crowd, ten years old, maybe, and his complexion has a blueish tint. He smiles at Liz.

"Who's the boy?"

"I think his name is Stevie," Emma says.

"Who's he with? Who would bring a child to a party like this?"

"I'm not sure."

"Why is his skin blue?"

"Is it?"

"Yes! Look at him."

"I really don't know much about him, dear. Do you want me to ask someone? I thought you wanted to meet Al."

"Fine, fine. Let's go."

They exit through a sliding door and head into the backyard. There's some party spillover out here—a few people standing around, smoking and talking—but nobody who fits the bill for Peora. Emma leads them to the center of the yard, toward what looks to be a clay sculpture. It's a life-size figure of a man with his arms outstretched. Sections of plaster are exposed through the clay, so it appears to be a work in progress. As they get closer, Liz can see that the details of the man's face are pretty crude. Still, if this is a hobby for Emma, it's not a bad eff—

"UGH! KICK ME IN THE CLIT!"

"Elizabeth! Watch your language."

That smell!

"What's that thing made of?" Liz asks, trying not to gag.

"That *thing?* Honestly! This is Al. He's made of BMs."

Liz holds her nose as she steps up to the sculpture. "This is your boyfriend?"

"The love of my life."

"Umm ... Well, okay. Are you gonna introduce me?"

Emma speaks to the sculpture. "Al, honey ... I'd like you to meet my daughter, Liz."

"I knew she was here the second she arrived," the statue replies, its mouth coming to life like some hideous Claymation character. "Even through all this shit, I could smell her rancid pussy."

Liz takes a step back, half-expecting Peora to reach out and grab her. But only his mouth keeps moving. He speaks to her directly this time:

"I should have destroyed you as soon as you arrived in the World Village. I let my curiosity get the best of me. I wanted to know what you are, who had sent you. I wouldn't have bothered if I had known that you're nothing but the sad dream of a corporate stooge."

"I might have more up my sleeve than you think."

"I don't think so. A fireball here, a lightning bolt there. You're not worth my time, not with the way you're fucking up the continuum. Stupid cunt."

"Isn't he wonderful?" Emma says with a smile.

It's suddenly, painfully clear to Liz that Emma can't be helped. She's living in an illusion—seeing what she wants to see, hearing what she wants to hear. Liz isn't going to convince her to leave the World Village. She needs to turn her attention to Peora, needs to show him something new. But what ...? Liz recalls what the man in her cell told her:

I'm betting you can do ... hell, anything.

It's time for you to find out how powerful you really are.

Liz feels terrible that she never even got the guy's name. She has no doubt that she would still be in her cell if it wasn't for him. It would never have occurred to her that the laws of nature don't apply to her. That she can bend reality around herself with the force of her thoughts.

Think it and make it happen.

When she zapped the guard in her cell, she was thinking about one of Ryan's video games. Now, his comic books are coming to mind. She smiles. This could be interesting.

Liz gives Emma one last hug—a quick one, this time. "Think about going to the airport. Please. You're not going to want to be here soon. Trust me."

"What the fuck does that mean?" Peora asks.

Liz doesn't answer him. Instead, she takes one step back and delivers a spinning wheel kick to his nose.

"Take that, shit-for-brains."

Peora's head breaks off his body and sails through the air, all the way into the next yard, where it lands in a decorative sand garden. The head rolls several times, covering Peora's shit face with sand, before crashing against a statue of a meditating turtle.

The neighbor lady starts screaming.

Emma faints.

"Sorry. Gotta go," Liz says.

She launches herself into the air and flies away.

The camera POV is with Liz as she soars over the World Village, tattooed arms outstretched like Supergirl. Vantage point is low to the ground like a cruise missile. Liz's effect on her surroundings can no longer be questioned—things are changing before her eyes. The landscape below her is filled with dinosaur swamps one second and domed cities the next. She can taste sounds and hear colors. She has total sight, a transcendental view of the past and the future. She sees time as a track stretching out ahead of her, and she's riding it like a runaway train car. The track is a glowing ouroboros, circling the globe, looping back upon itself, devouring itself again and again. Those feelings of déjà vu weren't crazy. Liz has been here before, done this before. Her path is the same as always but different than it's ever been. Where will she end up this time? How will the world end up this time?

The World Village border wall is approaching fast. Accelerate to ramming speed! It's time to welcome some new residents to this quaint little burg. Some fresh blood to liven up the joint. Get ready for impact in:

Three ...

Two ...

One ...

Cut to a wide shot of the wall as Liz crashes through it. A thirty-foot section breaks away and crumbles into hundreds of boulder-sized chunks, kicking up a massive cloud of dust.

Cut to a medium-wide shot of the opening in the wall. ANSIS-infected zombies are coming through. Hundreds of them stumble over the boulders and shamble their way into the World Village. They look horrific, covered with bulging, bleeding tumors. "Brains!" one of them shouts. "Braaaaaaaains!"

"CUT! CUT! CUT!" Mitch yells.

Barry sidles up to his director/lover. "Problem, boss?"

"It looks like shit," Mitch says. "There's not enough bodies. Why so few extras? What's the story?"

"Same story as always. We put out a call for a hundred people. Sixty responded. Thirty showed up."

"Well, we need more. Grab whoever you can from the set. Where's Bell?"

"In his trailer. His next scene isn't until seven o'clock."

"Put that washed-up prima donna in some zombie makeup and get his ass out here. All hands on deck! It still won't be enough people, but if we layer the hell out of everybody, we might trick the audience into seeing a zombie horde."

"Okay, I'll get on it." He turns to leave.

"And, Barry?"

He stops, takes a moment to gather himself, and turns around. "Yes, boss?"

"Did you explain to them that these aren't George Romero-type zombies? That they're infected with syphilis?"

"Yes, I did."

"Run it down for them again. That moron in front was yelling for brains."

"Yes, boss." As Barry walks away, he reminds himself that Mitch is under a lot of pressure. Tempers are bound to flare up, especially with such a tight production schedule. He and Mitch have been joined at the hip for eighteen days now. Three more days and they'll be done. Well, not *done*—post-production will be grueling, too. But it's these fourteen-hour days on set that always test their professional/personal relationship the most. They'll get through it. They've made enough movies together to know that you have to grind it out. There's no way to rush it.

Some things take time.

CHAPTER 23

From the "In Concert" section of BurntheSystemDown.com:

THE BROWN UNDERGROUND – GORMAN FOUNDRY – CHICAGO, IL

I have mixed feelings about doing a concert review for the latest Brown Underground show. Calling one of their performances a "concert" is like calling D-Day a day at the beach. The Brown Underground is a combination of music, performance art, political activism, and overt chaos. The members refer to themselves as turd terrorists, and the impromptu locations where they perform are dubbed riot zones. If you think that description sounds over the top, think again.

The long-abandoned Gorman Foundry, lit only by oil drum bonfires, was the perfect backdrop for the Brown Underground's latest experiment in insanity. A crowd of more than 500 people was on hand, gathered below an elevated metal platform that served as the stage. They danced like it was the end of the world to the crushing EBM beats provided by Elizabeth Herro, the Brown Underground's keyboardist/DJ. The other members (I counted as many as 28 performers on the platform at one time) used found objects to augment Herro's electronics. This included sections of rebar, wrenches, sheet metal, crucibles, metal buckets and chain hoists. The songs reflected the group's fight-shit-with-shit attitude, including electro-industrial thumpers like "Lying Sack of Shit" and "Can't Shit a Shitter." A huge projection screen showed clips of scat porn videos. A dozen or so performers channeled their inner GG Allin and took a crap on stage. They also rubbed the feces on themselves like war paint and battled each other with chainsaws and flamethrowers.

As crazy as all of this was, you knew that things would be taken to another level at some point. This happened at about the 90-minute mark when a large, tarp-covered object was wheeled into the crowd. The unveiling revealed a human gyroscope ride, the kind you see at carnivals and state fairs. Strapped into the device was Brandon Stockman, the CEO of Cybersquare Inc., who had gone missing two days earlier. Stockman, of course, is best known for buying himself a $950,000 diamond-inlaid business suit the same week he initiated massive layoffs at Cybersquare.

He was strung up wearing that very suit in the gyroscope.

Herro announced that Stockman had been given a potent laxative. As she launched into "Cut the Crap," one of the Brown Underground's most popular songs, the gyroscope was set in motion. The idea was to play the song as long as necessary, keeping the CEO in constant motion until he shit his pricey britches. Those hoping for an extended dance mix were disappointed as diarrhea began flying in all directions after only a minute. Those hoping to see a rich asshole get humiliated in public went home very, very happy.

An interesting side note: There were a lot of rumors going around that night that a First Response Assault Team was going to raid the show. The Brown Underground was prepared for this contingency with loads of water balloons filled with sewage and ready to toss. But the FRAT boys never showed up. A spontaneous protest at the courthouse that evening may have diverted them. I think it's just as well they were MIA. Several members of the Brown Underground were armed, and I hate to think what might have happened if things had gone down wrong. As it was, this was an unforgettable performance representing one of the most important movements (no pun intended) of our time. -- Review by D.B.

From the SHITHOLE USA OFFICIAL STRATEGY GUIDE (BRADYGAMES SIGNATURE SERIES):

RETURN TO THE DUNG CENTER

The Choice Is Yours

After you watch the cut scene of Emma's flight departing, it's time for Liz to go back to the DUNG Center for a final confrontation with Belphegor. How she gets there is up to you. The teleportation point outside the airport is your fastest option. However, Liz's newly unlocked flight mode is a great way to survey the World Village and see if there are any side missions you want to complete. Refer to your on-screen mini-map as you fly around. The green marker is the DUNG Center, and the red markers are unfinished side missions.

Time to Stock Up!

When Liz arrives at the DUNG Center, be sure to explore the outside grounds before entering the building. A thorough search yields the following:

-2 large med packs

-6 small med packs

-3 boxes of shotgun shells
-6 NitroJet-x rounds
-10 pistol clips
-6 hand grenades

Refer to the map on page 129 of this guide for the exact location of these items. You're going to need all of them for what lies ahead!

Lobby

As soon as Liz enters the DUNG Center lobby, a swarm of guards emerges from the station at the back of the room. Take cover or die! There are multiple cover options in the front part of the lobby, including pillars, large planters, and furniture. Lean out, aim, and fire when the opportunity presents itself. If you stay in one place for too long, your cover object takes heavy damage, so you need to duck and roll to multiple positions. As always, Liz's Inazuma lightning strike is your most effective weapon. However, its recharge time is a detriment in this battle. Alternate between using Inazuma and other weapons to defeat the guards.

Guard Station

When the lobby fight ends, explore the now-empty guard station to find the following items:

-1 small med pack
-3 pistol clips
-First Floor Map
-Prison Officer's Journal
-Microchip implant gun

Next to the filing cabinet is a machine that programs the DUNG Center's employee microchips. The machine is locked with a four-digit passcode. To learn the passcode, read the Prison Officer's Journal. There are four entries, and each one includes a numerical reference:

-Entry 1: One new employee

-Entry 2: Nine circles of Hell
-Entry 3: Six prisoners in solitary confinement
-Entry 4: Eight days until the Change begins
The passcode is 1968.

Once you unlock the microchip machine, follow the on-screen prompts to program a chip for Liz. Be sure to give Liz the highest security clearance (Level 5). Then go to your inventory and combine the completed chip with the microchip implant gun. A cutscene plays, showing Liz shooting the chip into her forehead. When the cutscene concludes, you can move freely throughout the DUNG Center. Discard the microchip implant gun; Liz is done with this item, and there's no reason to waste one of your inventory slots.

Hell on Earth

Examine the First Floor Map. Note that the Laboratory Elevator is circled in green. This is Liz's next destination—begin making your way there. As with most indoor environments, your on-screen mini-map isn't available, so stop and recheck the First Floor Map as needed. As you progress, the lights in the facility start to flicker, sometimes going out entirely. During these blackout moments, send an Inazuma lightning strike down the hall for illumination. As Liz gets closer to the elevator, pentagrams and other Satanic symbols are scrawled on the walls in blood. Demon imps begin to materialize; the best way to defeat them is with a couple of shotgun blasts.

Going Down

When you finally reach the elevator, get in and take the long ride to the bottom. Exit the elevator and explore the Underground Laboratory. Numerous doors are marked with Satanic symbols. Does one of them lead to Belphegor? There's no way to know, because Liz's attempts to enter result in an error message saying that Level 6 security clearance is required. Uh-oh! Level 5 isn't the highest level? What's Liz going to do?

There's only one door you can enter: the one marked "Primate Research Facility." Go inside and search the intake area to find the Animal Tech's Journal. There are several entries from Betty-Jo describing the atrocities committed at the research facility. The final entry is the most important, as it describes Betty-Jo's plans to free the animals and sabotage the operation. Go to the far end of the intake area and enter the door marked "Subject 1: Sleep Deprivation."

Subject 1: Sleep Deprivation

A crazed chimpanzee bounds about the room. Be prepared to dodge his frantic lunges. It's possible to make a mad dash past the chimp to the next door, which is marked "Subject 2: Cross-Breeding." Don't do this! You'll need to come back this way, and it's important to take care of this enemy now. Your weapons don't affect the deranged beast, not even Liz's Inazuma lightning strike, which only stuns the chimp for a few moments. The key is to use Inazuma and a weapon in tandem. Hit the chimp with Inazuma, and while he's weakened, blast him as many times as possible with your weapon of choice. You need to repeat this process several times to put him down. You can then proceed to the next room.

Subject 2: Cross-Breeding

Get ready for an even bigger, badder beast: the ape-o-dile. He's looking to take a bite out of Liz. Chompity-chomp! Use the same stun-and-gun technique you employed with Subject 1. Be forewarned: It's more challenging this time around because you have the creature's swinging crocodile tail to contend with.

Once you've dispatched the ape-o-dile, investigate the noises coming from the storage locker. You discover Betty-Jo hiding in there. A cutscene plays, and Betty-Jo gives Liz some of the answers she's been searching for. She explains that ANSIS was created here, under Peora/Belphegor's direction, and infected hosts were released into Florida's general population. This was done to keep the World Village as isolated as possible and ensure Peora's influence over the residents. Their fecal worship gives him power, and he's almost ready to unleash his master plan, something called "The Change." If he succeeds, America will be transformed into a world of poop. Betty-Jo also reveals that she has Level 6 security clearance, which means she can unlock the door that leads to Belphegor's lair.

More Monkey Business?

Several more subjects await you in the rooms ahead:

-Subject 3: Radiation Treatment

-Subject 4: Steroid Treatment

-Subject 5: Hypnosis

-Subject 6: Rage Induction

These are side missions that have no bearing on the main campaign. Complete them if you're in the mood for more ape-blasting action (you'll be rewarded with a few health and ammunition items). Otherwise, retrace your steps to the main hallway. Betty-Jo follows along with you.

NOTE: If you didn't kill Subject 1, the ape rips Betty-Jo to shreds as soon as you re-enter the Sleep Deprivation room. Game over!

Portal to Hell

When you reach the main hallway, Betty-Jo leads Liz to the correct door and unlocks it. There's a glowing orange vortex inside. Step into it and get ready for one Hell of a fight!

Final Boss Fight: Belphegor

You're transported to Hell, a landscape of flames, erupting volcanos, and rivers of lava. You stand in the middle of a giant pentagram that takes up the entire ground of the playfield. Just outside the pentagram, Belphegor sits on his toilet throne. The five points of the pentagram begin to glow, one at a time, randomly. You need to make your way to each glowing point—these are the only five places where you can inflict damage on Belphegor. The King of Waste has three tactics to impede your progress:

-Shit Golems: Belphegor sends wave after wave of these shitty creatures at you. Use your NitroJet-x rounds to turn them into flaming piles of poo.

-Diarrhea: Be ready to dodge the brown torrents that overflow from Belphegor's toilet and threaten to sweep you away.

-Fart Blasts: You can't dodge Belphegor's noxious shockwaves. The only way to avoid them is with a carefully timed double-jump. If you're not precise, you'll take heavy damage.

When you reach a glowing pentagram point, match the button command sequence that appears on the screen to launch an animated super attack. After you execute a super attack from each point of the pentagram, Belphegor falls in defeat.

Roll Credits

Your campaign has come to an end. Some mysteries have been solved, and others may never be explained. When the end credits conclude, the game automatically opens Shitstorm Mode, which allows you to replay *Shithole USA* at a 10x difficulty level.

From the July 7, 1986, edition of the CHICAGO TRIBUNE:

Chicago Boy, 10, Suffocates in Refrigerator at Aunt's

The body of a 10-year-old Chicago boy, who apparently suffocated, was found in a refrigerator in the garage of his aunt's North Side home late Saturday, the police said yesterday.

The boy, Stephen Tinker, and his parents were visiting the boy's aunt at 1968 W. Oak Street. They last saw him playing outside at 3 p.m. Saturday afternoon, according to Officer Anthony Kent, a spokesman for the police. At 4:30 p.m., they noticed he was missing and began searching the neighborhood. At 10 p.m., the boy's father, Beauford Tinker, a sergeant in the U.S. Army, reported to the police that his son was missing.

While waiting for the police to arrive at the aunt's home, Sgt. Tinker began searching the garage. At 10:30 p.m., he opened the refrigerator, which was not working because of a broken compressor, and found the body of his son, his only child.

The police have surmised that the boy climbed into the old-model refrigerator, which could not be opened from the inside, and suffocated. Officer Kent said the medical examiner's office had yet to determine the exact cause of death.

CHAPTER 24

In a forest clearing, hundreds of chimpanzees dance around a raging bonfire, celebrating the destruction of the World Village and the Primate Research Facility. They blow horns and bang on drums. Fireworks light up the night sky. The Dragon Lady does a victory roll overhead. LANCE and ANDRE join in the revelry, moonwalking and breakdancing among the chimps. Emma and Betty-Jo are dancing with them, both doing a spirited version of the twist.

Liz laughs and claps to the beat as she watches the festivities. Also looking on are the ghostly forms of Ryan, Hank, and Stevie. The three glowing spirits smile at Liz, and she smiles back. Emma breaks from the party and joins Liz; the two of them embrace.

All is right in Liz's world.

Everything is just as it should be.

Okay, let's begin. First question: When you have a bowel movement, do you look at the toilet paper after you wipe?

... WISH YOU WERE HERE

Tinker concludes his presentation. The screen behind him goes dark, and the overhead lights come back on. "So that's the plan, ladies," he says. "Any questions?"

Count Dracula lifts a long, manicured nail. "My only concern is that—"

"I didn't ask if you had any concerns! I asked if you had any questions."

"Forgive me, but I don't think it's unreasonable to have trepidations about this friend of yours. This ... *Shatley*." The Count spits out the word like it's a chunk of garlic in his mouth. "The success of the whole affair rests with him, and none of us have made his acquaintance."

"*I've* made his acquaintance, you prissy fuck! I'm vouching for him. That's all you need to know."

"Very well," the Count says, backing down as usual (all bark, no bite). "If everyone else is fine with ... *Shatley* ... I shall capitulate."

"Capitulate *this,*" Tinker says, grabbing his crotch. Then he addresses the rest of the room: "Are we good? Should I get in touch with Shatley?"

All eyes shift to Hugh Lioli, the CEO of TekCircle Corporation. Lioli hasn't said a word yet. He's been sitting motionless throughout the meeting in his black robe and deer skull mask, complete with a full set of antlers. SOIL is run by majority rules. *In theory.* But in actuality, no one in the syndicate would consider moving ahead on something like this without Lioli's blessing, not even Tinker.

Lioli removes his mask and sets it on the conference table, making it look like a weird candelabra. He runs a hand through his thick red hair. "We move forward. The plan is solid, and if Mr. Tinker believes that Shatley is the right man for the job, that's good enough for me. It's strange, though. Something about him ... Those photos—he reminds me of that actor. What was his name? He sang that song ..." Lioli drifts away, humming a few notes of a phantom tune. He hears the words in his head:

The pulse
Yeah, you've got the pulse
Of Miami

Lioli snaps out of it. He seems irritated with himself. "Fuck it. It doesn't matter. Shatley is our man. He doesn't remind me of anyone."

ABOUT THE AUTHOR

Mark Zirbel is the Wonderland Award-nominated author of Cyberpunk Zombie Jihad, which BiffBamPop.com calls "an absurdist, industrial, horror, sci-fi short story collection of doom." Mark's bizarro, cyberpunk, and horror fiction has been published in dozens of anthologies and magazines and was most recently featured in The Blind Dead Ride Out of Hell (St Rooster Books), Zombie Punks Fuck Off (CLASH Books/Weirdpunk Books), and Strange Behaviors: An Anthology of Absolute Luridity (NihilismRevised). Mark has self-published two chapbooks: Notes on the Propagation of Angels (A User Guide) and Double Maim Event: Two Tales of Mat-Slamming Horror. His story "Bags" received an honorable mention in the 20th edition of The Year's Best Fantasy & Horror (St. Martin's Press). Shithole USA is Mark's debut novel.

OTHER TITLES FROM PLANET BIZARRO

Peculiar Monstrosities – A Bizarre Horror Anthology

A stripper's boyfriend bites off more than he can chew during a hiking trip.
A man looking for love marries a jukebox.
A popular children's character is brought to life, but something isn't quite right.
A shady exchange on a Kaiju cruise leads to catastrophic complications.

Peculiar Monstrosities is packed with fourteen exquisitely crafted stories from new and established authors of Bizarro fiction.

Featuring tales by: Kevin J. Kennedy, Zoltan Komor, Shelly

Lyons, Tim Anderson, Tim O'Neal, Gregory L. Norris, Joshua Chaplinsky, Stanley B. Webb, Jackk N. Killington, Kristen Callender, Michael Pollentine, Tony Rauch, Mark Cowling, and Alistair Rey.

Extremely Bizarre – A Bizarro/Extreme Horror Anthology

A lonely man gets more than he bargained for after ordering a hand-in-a-can from an old magazine.

Enter a world where face pareidolia is deadly and one mistake can lead to a horrifying death.

Join a traumatized woman as she returns to the place of her son's death, looking for something to fill the hole in her life.

Extremely Bizarre is an exquisite collection of ten tales accompanied by detailed illustrations.
Expect extreme horror. Expect bizarro. Expect therapy.

Featuring tales by: Robert Guffey, Shaun Avery, Sergi G. Oset, Kevin J. Kennedy, T.M. Morgan, Irene Ferraro-Sives, Cliff McNish, B. Patrick Lonberg, Todd Love, Melanie Atkinson, and Gerard Houarner.

Sons of Sorrow

by Matthew A. Clarke

SOME THINGS ARE BETTER LEFT ALONE

Henk has been living a relatively carefree life in the city since fleeing the horrors of the town of Sorrow with his brother, Dave. Never would he have dreamt of returning. Not even for her.

But time and banality have a funny way of eroding the memory of even the worst experiences, bringing only the better times to the forefront of recall, so when he receives a wedding invitation from the third part of their old monster-fighting trio, he finds himself unable to turn it down.

Sorrow has changed drastically from the place it once was, with the murders and suicides that once plagued the town being used as a selling point by wealthy investors to turn it into a morbid attraction for dark tourists.

Beneath the costumed mascots and smiling families, is all really as it seems? Or by returning, have Henk and Dave inadvertently awoken an ancient evil far deadlier than anything they've faced before?

Sons of Sorrow is the latest bizarre horror from the mind of Matthew A. Clarke.

Porn Land

By Kevin Shamel

OH, NO, PORN IS ILLEGAL!

That's right. Porn stars are criminals, pornographic websites are being systematically destroyed, and not even softcore or selfies are okay. And that's just in our world. It's literally destroying the magick city of sexual expression—PORN LAND!

Phil and Zed, arriving through magickal means and ill-equipped for adventure, must travel through the erotic metropolis and gather pieces of THE PORNOMICRON—a sexual spell-book that bridges our worlds. And it won't be easy. They'll have to get past a giant geisha and her samurai army, a determined detective who's after their asses, a badass dominatrix and her gang, a bunch more sexy people, a bunch of unsexy people... And even more things that will freak you out and make you horny—like a sperm monster and ambulance sex. Will Phil and Zed put the book together, save Porn Land and their new friends, *and* make pornography legal in our world again? (Yes. It'd be a stupid story if they didn't. But it's *how* they do it that you'll want to read about.)

It's a story about sucking, *and* not sucking. It's got hardcore sex *and* a hardcore message. It's ridiculous *and* you'll wanna rub one out to it. It's freakin' PORN LAND, BABY!

Weird Fauna of the Multiverse

A trio of novellas by Leo X. Robertson

— A gimp becomes mesmerized by the koala at a zoo on Venus. She draws him into the battle between the purebred animal supremacy of the park's hippo owner and the anti-establishmentarian koala uprising.

— In a godless future, a rich Martian traveler hunts the former Vatican–now a hotspot for sex tourism—for his deceased wife. When he discovers a dead priest in the streets, he begins to investigate the weird plot of the city's head cyberpope.

— Supercats spend their days responding to rescue calls across their city. Since there aren't enough rescues to go around, one supercat decides to do something drastic and devious to resolve this crisis, changing the industry forever.

The stories of *Weird Fauna of the Multiverse* explore what happens to love and work when pushed beyond the boundaries of human decency.

A Quaint New England Town

by Gregory L. Norris

When Ezra Wilson took the job as a census worker, he never imagined it would lead to a place like his latest assignment. From the moment he turns off the interstate and travels past the village limits, it becomes clear that Heritage isn't just some quaint New England town.

A sinister encounter at an automobile graveyard is only the start. In Heritage Proper, a town divided down the middle both politically and literally, Ezra is met with hostility on both sides of an imposing brick wall that separates warring factions that have maintained a fragile peace. After scaling the wall into Heritage North, Ezra discovers a beautiful young woman held prisoner in a fortified basement room and promises to help her. To do so will expose the last of the small town's dark secrets and lay bare big planetary dangers if Ezra survives his visit to a destination where even the white picket fences are not at all what they appear to be.

Russells in Time
by Kevin Shamel
Because you can never have enough Shamel! In this novella, a trio of recognizable characters find themselves travelling back in time and in the middle of a heated battle between the dinosaurs and a race of giant land-squid. Who will they side with? And will we get to see Russell Brand kicking ass in an Iron Man-esque suit? (Spoiler — yes. We totally will.)

Selleck's 'Stache is Missing!
by Charles Chadwick

Celebrated Hollywood star Tom Selleck has it all: talent, good looks, a winning personality, and a track record of television and movie hits, enjoyed by millions around the world. Until one day, while filming his latest project, an old rival attacks him and steals his mustache. Now, lost and adrift, Tom struggles with his new life. Along with a group of dedicated crew members, celebrity friends, government agents, and the robot voice of an old co-star, he has to find the strength to take on his greatest role ever: tracking down his old rival, retrieving his legacy, and saving the world.

Songs About My Father's Crotch

by Dustin Reade

My father's crotch sang many songs, and the first of them all, was me.

Now it is my turn to sing, and I will sing to you of many things. Here are my stories. Here are my songs.

I will sing of a man who wrestles furniture, and of a sister who disappears.

I will sing of modern day cannibalism, and Dwayne Johnson's elbow.

I will sing of foul-mouthed butterflies and plastic sharks, and I will hum a few bars about cartoon trains.

I will warble on about beards, sentient houses, monsters and Roald Dahl.

But mostly, with this collection of short stories, I will sing songs about my father's crotch.

Bizarro outsider, Dustin Reade, presents eleven stories of weirdo lit, culled from the deepest recesses of the human imagination, and sprinkled with thoughts and flakes from other parts of the body as well.

Don't miss it. Or do. Whatever.

The Secret Sex Lives of Ghosts
by Dustin Reade

Thomas Johansson can see ghosts after a near death experience, and has made a living killing them for a second time. After discovering that being possessed by a ghost causes an intense hallucinogenic effect, he goes into business with a perverted dead man named Jerry, selling possession as a street drug (street name: Ghost). But is the farmhouse he sees while possessed really a hallucination? Or is it something else?

The Falling Crystal Palace
by Carl Fuerst

The residents of Sterling, Indiana don't know who they are. Sixty-one year old Tory Stebbins runs an Identity Verification agency that can help. But, as her town implodes, so does her business. She has fewer clients, stiffer competition, and her methods have become mysteriously ineffective. Most alarmingly, she's now suffering from the same problems she's helped her clients with over the length of her career.

Just when her situation seems beyond hope, Tory receives a cryptic message from Hoppy Bashford, her best friend who, forty years earlier, disappeared. "I don't want to say it's a life or death situation," writes Hoppy, "but I want to say it's a life or death situation."

Tory's quest to find Hoppy leads her through the strange, shifting landscapes of Sterling, and the enigmatic quarry around which it is built, and ultimately to the Crystal Palace Resort, a hotel and waterpark with an infinite maze of hallways, rooms, and bizarrely themed attractions whose size and scope defy physics and reason. To locate her lost friend, escape from the resort, and find a cure for the identity-scrambling, reality-bending condition from which everyone in her world suffers, Tory must come to terms with who she is; she must determine her place in, relationship to, and path through the universe.

Dead Monkey Rum
by Robert Guffey
A mixture of urban fantasy and Los Angeles noir, *Dead Monkey Rum* revolves around a stolen Tiki idol that contains the ashes of visionary artist Stanislaw Szukalski. Our heroes, an alcoholic monkey named Robert McLintock and a beautiful bartender named Stephanie Waterfall, must locate the missing statue in the wilds of Los Angeles before a tribe of pissed-off Yetis can get their massive, dirty paws on it. Because the obsidian idol possesses magical properties, the Yetis want to use it to kickstart the destruction of the human race, thus paving the way for the cryptozoological beasts to take humanity's place as the rulers of Earth.

Ebola Saves the Planet! and Other Wholesome Tales
by Matthew A. Clarke
A man gets a ticket to a popular gameshow and is willing to risk life and limb to go home with the prize.

A family tries to survive in a world where gravity is reversed and explosive balloon animals rule the streets.

A new epidemic hits the world. People are spontaneously erupting into mounds of steel coils, but after years, the kids are growing restless. Will they be able to survive a secret outing outside of their safehouse?

A young girl born to super villains feels out of place among her family and peers. Upon discovering a dastardly plot to cause widespread catastrophe, will she defy her family and save the planet?

Ebola Saves the Planet! and Other Wholesome Tales is a collection of eleven wild tales (and illustrations) from the mind of Matthew A. Clarke.

Lightning Source UK Ltd.
Milton Keynes UK
UKHW040633301122
413118UK00004B/201